CADENCE

Book Two of The Waterblaze Trilogy

BY CHINA DENNINGTON

First edition.

Double Eagle Media
4400 N Scottsdale Rd, #9129
Scottsdale, AZ
85251

Library of Congress Control Number: 2019900061

ISBN-13: 978-0-9907274-5-3

TABLE OF CONTENTS

Chapter One	3
Chapter Two	19
Chapter Three	25
Chapter Four	37
Chapter Five	55
Chapter Six	66
Chapter Seven	76
Chapter Eight	89
Chapter Nine	91
Chapter Ten	103
Chapter Eleven	110
Chapter Twelve	117
Chapter Thirteen	124
Chapter Fourteen	130
Chapter Fifteen	132
Chapter Sixteen	142
Chapter Seventeen	158
Chapter Eighteen	161
Chapter Nineteen	163
Chapter Twenty	170

Chapter Twenty-One   177

Chapter Twenty-Two   184

Chapter Twenty-Three   188

Chapter Twenty-Four   194

Chapter Twenty-Five   201

Chapter Twenty-Six   205

Chapter Twenty-Seven   210

Chapter Twenty-Eight   224

Chapter Twenty-Nine   227

Chapter Thirty   235

Chapter Thirty-One   240

Chapter Thirty-Two   251

Chapter Thirty-Three   257

Epilogue   263

The merwoman screamed as much out of fear as of pain. The contractions grew stronger and she felt her daughter emerging from her body like a storm ripping through a forest. She prayed desperately for the child's survival. *I can't stand to lose one more.* Her husband squeezed her hand as with one last push the baby slid into the water.

The mother's breath caught as she saw the paleness of her sweet daughter's face as the cord was cut. The doctor stood staring at the little girl with his mouth twisted in barely concealed disgust.

"I can't lose another," the mother muttered.

"Something is wrong. Help her!" she screamed at the apathetic doctor.

He shrugged.

"Her heart is weak. I'm sorry, but as a sixteen she doesn't have the level of medical coverage necessary to save her. Better off this way anyways."

The mother scooped up her child and brought her soft, clammy skin to her own. She locked eyes with the doctor and spit, "I am a one and my daughter will survive. If she doesn't, you will answer to the royal courts. Consider carefully. You know a three won't win against a one."

Elaina hated using the class card. But when her healthy, live daughter was handed back to her hours later, she didn't regret it. "Don't ever let anyone tell you that you have a weak heart, Astrid," she whispered, stroking the child's innocent face.

CHAPTER ONE

Astrid stared down at her scientific notetablet. She pushed her thin red stylus against the screen, frustration cramping her fingers. Sighing, she looked up towards space through the water, pushing strands of rich, ruby-colored hair out of her face and gathering them into a side ponytail.

She didn't want to move. Her thoughts felt crowded, suffocating and she wanted to sort them out. But she also knew that moving would make her feel better. Besides, she couldn't let two months of work go to waste.

She made herself get up off the assortment of smooth blue and purple rocks that spread for miles around her. The plain of colorful stones felt like it was swallowing her up in its vastness. She could make out only two things; the outline of

the city in the distance, and, of course, her six
monitoring devices only a short swim away.

Astrid finally reached the stout, waist-high
cylinders halfway buried in the smooth pebbles.
Reaching out, she touched one. The slight buzz
jumped through her hand, and through her body
to a lesser extent. *Temperature: Just right.*

She'd set up these sensors weeks ago to
monitor the activity of the core. Something no
other Akaytan scientist was doing. The sensors
sent out various signals to the core that took
readings then boomeranged them back.

Astrid glanced around nervously out of habit.
She felt lucky no one had discovered her project.
She didn't even want to think about what would
happen if the experiment was traced back to her.
That was one part of her life she never examined
too closely: what would happen if her scientific
activities were discovered.

The logical part of her mind knew that she
had no reason to be worried about their
discovery. No one she'd ever known dared, or
even desired, to travel outside of Akayta.

A pang of sorrow hit her stomach. At least
no one she knew now.

The devices were measuring the cycles of the
melions inside the rock core of her planet. This
experiment hadn't been done in centuries. That's

what made it so intriguing to her. The melions: particles inside the core that shrank and grew with a rhythm. If that rhythm ever got thrown off kilter, the core would shatter. And if the core shattered, then the center of gravity of the water planet would be destroyed and the water would disperse into space.

Of course, the possibility of the melions getting out of rhythm was only a theory. It would probably never happen. Among other things, she was measuring the core's temperature, pressure, and water content.

Geology had always been one of her favorite branches of science. Astrid spent hours on end in her room, hunched in her closet, studying rock fragments under her portable light. Even though her room was in the center of her large house, and she was the only one living in it, she always felt safer conducting her experiments in her large closet.

Her sister, Effie, was technically the one who owned her dead parents' house, but she allowed Astrid to continue to reside there. That was one thing the mergirl was grateful for. Effie had every right as the owner of the house, and a firstborn, to send her to the area fondly referred to as the double digit sector.

She had passed through the sector just that morning. It was small, confined to the boundaries that the royal family set, no matter how the population grew. The cluster of one-room huts sagged so much they appeared to sink into the sand itself. Dark, devoid of variation, crowded. Abandoned children sat caked in salt and mud, absentmindedly drawing in the sand.

A young girl had locked eyes with her as she passed. The hopelessness was as apparent as the dirt on her face. Her clothes—little more than loose fabric—were too small, and she quickly broke eye contact in fear and shame. The stench in the water was nearly unbearable. Too many bodies packed into a small space.

She'd seen double digits as young as eight and nine years old living there alone. Some parents just didn't want to deal with the shame of having a person of such a low number in their household. So they'd ship them off to the double digit sector. There was no one to take care of them, or the older ones for that matter. That's why they lived in such poverty. When they were old enough to obtain a job, the work would barely pay for food.

Most people hurried past the double digit sector and frowned on it with scorn. But Astrid wasn't one of those people. She knew she could've easily been relegated to living there. Most others wouldn't give a second thought to how the outcasts survived, or their responsibility for those living conditions. But Astrid slowed down each time she passed through it, and watched how many of the outcasts, with their meager victuals, would share with the others.

The double digits were always hungry, but most survived. She didn't want to think about how many children would die if that spirit of commiseration wasn't present. And most single digits didn't even care. What was meant to deny their humanity had only amplified it.

She turned on her notetablet and glanced at the timer, which was counting down to the point when all data gathering would be complete.

Ten minutes. She had some time to think.

Astrid took a seat on the uncomfortable field of pebbles. She took a deep breath and then let it out. For a second she just focused on the feeling of water rushing in and out, giving her oxygen.

Her thoughts felt all jumbled. Closing her eyes, she tried to think clearly. When she turned seventeen, she would choose a job based on her mark. She wanted to be a scientist, but only the eldest siblings were allowed such a high-class job.

She was the sixteenth child. *I am a sixteen,* she thought, as though that would change the fact. The wish of being a firstborn, or maybe even a two or a three, was often present. But then she always felt guilty for wishing that. She believed there was nothing actually wrong with being born a sixteen. The mindset of Akaytan society was where the perversity entered the scene. When she wished to be something else, she felt as if she were abandoning her ideals.

The caste system all stemmed from the story that when the thirteen Sirof created the world, they poured the most intelligence, creativity, and aptitude into the first child of a family. They poured less into the second child, and so on and so forth. Fours or more only made it to the afterlife as servants.

She'd never bought into it. Astrid saw the system for exactly what it was, a religion designed to keep a caste system alive and thriving.

As a scientist, she was practical. She didn't believe in magic. When she looked at the beauty and complexity of the world around her, she knew it was created by something. It was scientifically impossible for all the right elements to come together in just the right way to create life and the universe by chance. She just didn't know what or who that creator was. It certainly wasn't the Sirof, though.

It wasn't easy being a sixteen. Even a lucky one. It was a common occurrence to be the object of disdainful glances and the target of cruel jokes. But she couldn't change who she was. She was only allowed to choose from jobs considered low-level, such as servant. *I will not be respected, none of my discoveries will be taken seriously. I cannot be a scientist, for it is against the law.* She wished she could cry, but she just felt numb. Numb about everything. Her future had no prospects, she only had life as the lowest class to look forward to. For her, the limit was way before the sky.

Astrid looked back down at her notetablet. Finally, the results were coming in.

A slight smile passed across her face as she remembered how she got the all-in-one science device. Her older sister Effie smuggled it to her when she found Astrid trying to do a test with makeshift materials and learned of her love for science. Perhaps out of guilt about her privileges, she chose to be a scientist to aid her sister in her endeavors. Since each scientist was given two notetablets, she gave one to Astrid. Now, whenever Astrid needed any other materials, she just asked Effie.

She ran her hand over the blue metallic surface. There were streaks where silver showed through the blue paint that had been scratched away by endless hours of use.

A clicking sound came from the device to remind her that it was still on. She looked at the purple bars and other data that covered the screen and began making notes.

After a while she reached the data about the melions. She hadn't been able to find much information on them before this experiment. Excitement thrummed through her veins as she examined it; a simple bar graph showing the size of the melions every hour over a period of a few weeks. The first bar stated that all of the melions were twenty micrometers wide. The second hour they were eleven micrometers wide. The third hour they were twenty micrometers wide again. The fourth hour they were eight micrometers wide. She stared at it for several minutes then muttered, "This isn't right."

The bars were growing farther apart with each passing day. They were moving unsteadily, while they should've been moving back and forth with a steady, predictable path. She looked at the results once more with disbelief, hoping she had made a mistake. Astrid rechecked the monitor settings...*all correct.*

She stared at the rocky ground that stretched farther than the eye could see. *The melions will continue to get more erratic each day. This means…* she glanced back down at her notetablet, doing the math. *It's going to explode in just a few weeks.*

Astrid felt like she was choking as she inputted the information to calculate the exact date. Swyn 27th at 3:48 in the afternoon.

Her heart pounded as she stared wide-eyed at the landscape without seeing it. This was her planet...her people. This would all be destroyed in just over six weeks. *I have to tell someone.* She swam upwards, her golden tail glistening as she snatched her notetablet and left hastily.

Nearing Akayta, Astrid could see several ships on their way to and from space. Though she couldn't see it from this distance, she knew the word *Oreclay* was scrawled across their sides. *Oreclay* was a government company focused on mining ore from nearby moons and asteroids.

Finally, she came into view of the city-state of Akayta itself. Its buildings were mainly a shiny white and black; pointed arches abounded. There was a respectable distance between all the buildings, though not too far. It felt airy, and none of the buildings were extremely tall. It was a city that gave you a sense of order and place. Nothing too dramatic. Even the Temple of the Sirof was relatively uniform.

One of the two areas that differed was the Palace Complex where the royal family of Akayta—supposedly the living incarnation of the Sirof—lived and worked. It rose in the middle of the city above all the other works of architecture.

It, too, was black and white. It was a structure with few curves (except for those of the pointed arches). It spread wide and was surrounded by a low, black and white striped wall made of painted bricks.

The only other place that broke the order was the double digit sector.

The wide streets gave way to a steady flow of merpeople swimming to and fro, but they weren't overly crowded. A few grey platforms—transports—carried metal in the travel lane. They were automated. Everyone dressed in simple clothes, each piece a single color. Many wore multi-strapped sleeves.

As she swam through the streets and over the white, fine sand her mind was flying. *Who should I tell?* Her heart raced as she tried to conjure up solutions. She stopped in the middle of the mainplace, a triangular area full of merpeople, shops, and businesses. *I could just shout it to everyone, it seems like they all need to know.* She dismissed the idea as soon as it entered her head. It just wasn't sensible. *No, no. That would just cause mass panic. I know, I'll tell Effie. Then Effie can get an audience with the royals.* Her sister worked as one of the royals' scientists, so she could speak with them.

Effie. The one relationship Astrid held onto. It was her anchor in life. Even though she was a sixteen, and therefore had fifteen siblings, they all died at birth except Effie. Her parents also died when she was very young. That left her extremely vulnerable as a child in a society that despised her.

The merpeople she sped past stared at her with disdain when they saw the red-and-black mark on her upper arm. It had been given to her at birth. Everyone had a mark. The numbered castes were color coded by group. Red-and-blacks were the most hated bracket. Her short sleeved, shiny silver top revealed the repulsive colors. She realized she left her jacket back at the test site. Showing up in public without a jacket was a mistake she rarely made, no matter how warm the water. But Astrid ignored the scorn. There were more important things to deal with. She sped up a little bit.

She arrived at a building that looked just like the others, but she'd been here so many times it was instinct, she didn't even have to look at the number on the door. Astrid hastily knocked. She heard the creak of a chair and a swish before the it slid open. Her eldest sister Effie stood there, her thick black eyebrows, long black hair, and ornery smile gave her a playful air. The golden mark on her arm swirled in triple loop triangle surrounded by a circle, the Akaytan symbol for one. Effie's smile fell when she saw the look on Astrid's face.

"What happened? What's the matter?"

Astrid glanced around at the passing hordes of merpeople and then hurried inside and closed the door behind her.

"What is it?" Effie asked.

Astrid's eyes radiated fear. She leaned against the door and closed her eyes, trying to gather her thoughts. Hesitantly turning on her notetablet, she handed it to Effie.

Astrid watched the disbelief grow on her sister's expressive face as she glanced over the data. Knowledge of melions was common, basic fact. So common, that most people would be able to interpret the data. Effie looked up with a tense seriousness that Astrid rarely saw from her. Effie's brown eyes held Astrid's bright blue ones.

"Are you sure that these results are accurate?"

"I wish they weren't."

That was all Effie needed, she grabbed her sister's hand and began to pull her. Astrid followed. She didn't need to ask where they were going, she already knew. The palace complex loomed as they drew closer. The disdainful glares continued as she swam with her sibling, but for the moment she ignored them. For all of her life she'd been their target, it didn't mean it didn't hurt, but sometimes it is better to focus on other things. Effie flashed a card by one of the guards on the other side of the gate. They nodded and pushed a button causing the gates to silently open. Effie rushed in, pulling Astrid with her.

She had never been in the palace except for once when she was a child. She winced at memories of intense judgmental glares and whispered words of disgust. Except for the royal family, all of the merpeople who lived or worked here were eldests. The gold insignias seemed to scream at her as they passed, people hurrying about or just chatting. Her older sister was used to it and was rather preoccupied, otherwise she would've been more considerate of Astrid's feelings. She focused on what was in front of her and tried to blur the people from her vision. Effie abruptly stopped at a large door that was being guarded.

"Are the royals assembled?" she asked.

The guard nodded sharply.

She swiped her card and said, "Emergency code clearance, priority one."

The guard, who up to this point had been composed in every movement, gaped in horror as he fumbled with the controls on his pad getting the door open. Effie didn't wait for the slick white doors with black swirling patterns on them to slide open all the way before entering. The five merpeople sitting on cushioned pedestals looked up as they entered. *The royals.* The oldest merman stood up and gave a curt nod.

"What is your news?" he asked. His bearing was regal and he wore bright, colorful garments, just as the rest of his family. His pedestal was the highest of the five, and on either side of his were two more. The ones directly on his left and right were lower than his, and the outer ones were the lowest. The brightly dressed royals wore silver arm bands and delicate silver crowns on their heads.

Astrid gaped. Effie nudged her. This was a nightmare that Astrid had thought would only ever be a fantasy. Facing the rulers of her kingdom, a sixteen. Would they scorn her too?

She swam closer and bent her tail back and her upper body forward in the equivalent of a mermaid curtsy. "Royals, I was doing a scientific experiment and I discovered that the melions in the core are beginning to fluctuate unsteadily and in six weeks the core will explode."

The king's eyes flew to her arm.

"What business do you have doing experiments? You're a sixteen, it's against the law," he said tersely.

"I know, but listen, if we don't do something then everyone is going to die."

The king didn't look like he was listening, he turned his eyes toward Effie, then they narrowed.

"Did you let this sixteen in—and did you know she was doing these tests outside of her caste?"

"Yes! But I strongly suggest, as one of your royal scientists, that you listen to her!" Effie said, emphasizing with her hands and trying to break through the king's limited point of view.

"Did you actually do the experiments?" he asked.

"No...but I've examined the results." Effie replied.

The king waved his hand dismissively.

"Spend no more time on this. Sixteens are always dishonorable. She likely faked the data." Astrid cringed. "Take her home with you. She will be dealt with this evening as she did break the law. But we currently have more important things to worry about than a wayward sixteen."

Astrid's face blushed with embarrassment and she was barely able to hold back her tears, "But it's true! In six weeks our planet will be destroyed and you will be sorry that you didn't listen to me. Just because I was born as the sixteenth child doesn't mean I'm dishonorable."

The king's face was starting to turn red.

"Come on," Effie whispered as she put her arm around her sister's shoulders and gently led her out of the room and through the palace.

Astrid's tears poured out of her eyes and into the equally salty surrounding ocean.

CHAPTER TWO

"What should I do, Effie?" Astrid moaned as she tried to get over the humiliation rushing through her. She looked around at the familiar apartment. This was her second home. The white walls and organized shelves might have looked cold to anyone else, but not to her. They were comforting in reminding her of her favorite sister's love. Which was ironic because Effie possessed everything Astrid had always wanted, everything she'd always dreamed of having.

The eldest mark, the opportunity to be a high-profile scientist. Respect. Astrid would never have any of these. The realization hit her all at once like a brick. She had known these facts her entire life, but now she truly understood. The pieces clicked. She would never be accepted as anything but a servant, she would never be treated with anything but disdain. There was no hope. Her heart burned with sadness.

It didn't matter anyway. She would be gone within six weeks now, her world forever shattered. Literally.

Astrid looked at the circular bright black-and-red emblem on her arm. A twisted circle made out the circumference, then within it a twisted infinity symbol held by a different looping circle. The symbol for sixteen.

Effie's normally playful face twisted with frustration as she stared at the notetablet, combing it over and over, hoping to find mistakes. Then after a few minutes of silence she slowly looked up at her sister and whispered, "You need to go."

Astrid's head whipped up in alarm and she stopped picking at her golden scales. "What?" she replied sharply.

Barely discernible bubbles floated off of Effie's eyelashes.

"You have to go. Soldiers will be coming soon to take you to prison. We...no, I, didn't think this through. I can't bear to see that. Besides, there are two other tribes. They must be warned."

Astrid recalled what little she knew about them. The two other tribes. Velee and Fillerra.

All three tribes used to be one nation called Atoa, but eventually they split because of a civil war. Each faction had a different idea about how the government should be run, and their disagreement was the planet's undoing. The Atoan war decimated much of Dalanda's ecology and wiped out the majority of the population. That was two hundred years ago. It was a rare occasion when they came into contact with each other. They all just let the others be, still painfully aware of their shared history.

Her mind snapped back to what Effie was saying. "Warn them, if not all the people will be saved, at least some of them will. Hopefully they will listen."

"No. I can't leave you here to die! I need you!" Astrid spoke frantically.

Her eyes softened and she tilted her head with a small smile. "No, you don't, baby sister. You don't need me. I have every confidence that you will be able to make it just fine. Don't worry about me, I will stay here and try to convince the royals that everyone needs to flee."

Effie got up out of her chair and briefly went into the other room. When she returned, she began opening and closing drawers as she put various items into a sack. Then, when she was done a few minutes later, she turned back to Astrid.

She thrust the small pack into her hands, "You have to go." She led her to the door. Astrid stared into her older sister's eyes with fear.

"What about…"

Effie calmly interrupted her. "You'll be fine. Now go. Go fast and don't let them catch you. Trust me, I've been to the prisons. You don't want to end up there."

As Effie shut the door Astrid couldn't tear her eyes away from her face. *This could be the last time I ever see her.* Her heart cried out as she slowly began to back away, then turned and sped through Akayta with her pack hidden under a jacket Effie gave her on the way out.

It was only a short time until she was out of the city, but every minute felt like an hour. Her eyes kept darting around looking for palace police or officials. Her heart pounded faster and faster. She felt like every single person was observing every little move she made. At least this time her insignia was hidden. Finally, just as the giant lamps that lit the city at night came on Astrid exited her city and her tribe, leaving behind her sibling and everything she'd ever known.

She was in a dusky area, the light from the city could just get to her and she knew that she would have to go farther tonight. Right? She sat down on the light brown, crystalline grains of sand on the south side of Akayta and dug through her bag until she found the lightcard. She turned it on and looked through the rest of her bag, since she hadn't really paid attention when Effie packed it for her.

She rummaged through it: food, water, necessities, and a coordinate director. It appeared that that was all she packed. Astrid closed her eyes, *How should I even begin trying to find them?* When she opened her eyes, the surrounding sea and sand just seemed bigger. She sighed, *I'd better get going.* She stood up, and as she did, began to repack the supplies.

As she was about to put the food back, she realized something. There was a small weight in the bottom of the bag. She reached inside and felt something smooth, small, and cold. She brought it out.

It was a silver disk. The outside shone bright like it had just been polished, but it seemed as if it also held the wisdom of age. She turned it in her hands and traced the intricate engraving of graceful twisting lines and flowers. As she ran her fingers over it, she noticed a bump on the rim. Astrid examined it more closely. It was a latch. *What is this?* It took a minute before she figured out how to unclasp it. Then it clicked. As she opened it, it felt like the water around her was just waiting to see what was held inside. It was silver on the inside as well, but there was no engraving. More importantly, there was something else folded neatly inside. She drew out the thick red slip of a flexible substance called palare. She gently unfolded it. Blue ink twirled around in Effie's beautiful handwriting:

42.62897, 34.25943 Travel to these coordinates, Astrid. They are the last recorded location of one of the other tribes. Whatever you do, don't let this fall into anyone else's hands. There is more to this than it seems. Hurry.

The message mystified Astrid as she read it over and over again. *There is more to this than it seems. What is she talking about?* After sitting there for a few more minutes she sighed. *Effie said to hurry and I've already spent too much time on this.* Astrid reluctantly closed the silver disk and replaced it in her pack. Then she switched on her coordinate director and turned to face the unknown.

CHAPTER THREE

The merman sat in a dark room with the high commander. His air was cool and confident...almost sinister. Black hair waved around a firmly set jaw and cutting green eyes.

The other merman's manner reeked of arrogance. The pomp etched into the lines of his face didn't make him look any younger. He crossed his arms and looked up impatiently. "Well, what do you want. I have a meeting in five minutes."

The first man smirked. "From now on you will take your orders from me. When I tell you to draft a new law, you will comply. When I tell you to commute a sentence, it will be done.

The high commander scoffed, "Do you know how ridiculous you sound? You have no power over me."
He started to get up when a slight smile lit up the first man's face, as if he knew something the other didn't.

"As I see it, you have two choices. One, you follow my orders, and then I give you the coordinates to a paradisal planet when I determine you are ready. Or two," here his eyes glinted with a dangerous light, *"I will have you assassinated before the end of the day. Besides, have you heard of Cog?"*

"The weapons inventor? Of course," he said, tension edging into his voice .

"He works for me now. I wouldn't disobey if I were you. The weapon he made will wipe out all of Velee in an instant. You are the high commander of Velee...and now you answer to me if you want to keep your life."

A cold fear pierced the high commander's heart at the calculating insanity in the other man's eyes. But he laughed, raising his eyebrows with a false confidence.

"You couldn't kill me even if you wanted to."

The first man smiled sickeningly as he leaned forward, "Yes, I can. My assassins surround you. You'll never know who they are until it's too late."

The high commander paled and stuttered under his breath, "You're behind the political assassinations."

The first man smiled, "You will report to me at these coordinates." He got up, handing him a piece of palare. He began to swim away and then stopped, turning his head back. *"If you betray me, you die."*

He swam away, leaving the high commander of Velee sitting frozen in fear.

~

Time seemed to stand still as her lightcard flickered off.

"No!" she grunted as she was left in complete darkness except for the almost indiscernible glow of her coordinate director. Astrid sat down on the sand, which had changed to a deep red color as she got further from her tribe, and huddled up, her tail aching. She stared at it trying to see its golden hue through the blackness.

Her tail color was rare. Dalandian tails came in many shades. From deep green, to stunning magenta and indigo, but few had golden tails. It was another factor that made her unique. Something that people weren't used to seeing. Red-and-blacks were the most looked down upon of all Akaytans, but they were also a small part of the population. On average, Akaytans had four children. The ones who did have many children, lost many as well. Due to their biology, mermaids who had more kids were also the ones who usually lost at least half of them at birth. *But I still have the mark, even though fourteen of my siblings died at birth. I'm part of a special class designated for the expression of hatred.*

She'd been traveling for hours now. It seemed like the night would never end. The coordinates were surprisingly close. She was only a few hours away from them now. Even the stars, which were usually shining bright, were covered by a storm in the upper atmosphere. Astrid felt like she was cut off completely from the world as she sat in the darkness. It seemed to press in on her, so she closed her eyes— not that it helped any. *Which tribe am I going to? And how can we not have been in contact with them for hundreds of years when they are this close? Well, we always have been a selfish people, not caring to look at anyone but ourselves,* she thought sarcastically. That was the way most people in Akayta appeared to her, even if she herself wasn't that way. She looked down at her coordinate director. Travel was still possible, but she decided that it was better to rest and wait for the piercing light of day. The stage of her mind gave way to a memory as she slept.

She was fifteen once again. She kept her head down as she swam across the path to another black and white home full of arches that looked exactly like her own. Even though she'd been careful to wear a cloak today, the people who knew her gave her looks of scorn as she passed. It was always this way, but that didn't make it any less painful. She quickly banished the thoughts from her head and tried to focus on where she was going. When she reached the door it opened immediately. The merboy inside eagerly motioned her in. His face was serious, but held a soft smile, his unruly strands of black hair floating slightly away from the top of his head. She looked toward the insignia on his arm that she'd seen so many times before. The red-and-black circle had a twisting x inside with a line through the middle. Eleven. Astrid lifted her head and smiled.

"We could go visit in the coral field today," he said.

Her smiled faltered as she looked toward the door. "That's a long way to swim."

"I understand," he said as he briefly glanced at his mark and then hers. "We can just read then."

Rune had been reading to her out of a science book for hours. That was about the best education that red-and-blacks could get. They were taught the basic skills of reading and writing, then left on their own. Astrid looked wistfully at the ceiling, these experiments and how everything worked was so fascinating. "I wish I could be a scientist. You know how I love it," she said suddenly, interrupting Rune. He looked at her with a spark of determination in his eyes. He focused on her intensely and took her hands. "Never forget this Astrid, you can be anything you want. Anything. Don't let that restrict you," he pointed to her mark. A fire burned in his eyes.

After that day she never saw him again. He simply disappeared, which was unheard of in Akayta— at least in the history that she remembered. She cried for months. The only person that ever treated her as an equal besides Effie. All of her other siblings and parents had died. Where was he? Was he okay?

Astrid woke with a start panting and could feel her heart accelerating. She put her head in her hands. The memory of the day that Rune disappeared was so clear. The dream haunted her. Even though it had been almost two years, tears started to leak out of her eyes and disperse into the surrounding water.

She turned her face toward the white sun. She'd once read that it was the brightest star they'd ever found with their space searching instruments. One thing was certain, it showed clearly through the water atmosphere.

Dalanda. She wasn't sure if she loved or hated the name of her planet. She loved the planet itself, but the people were cruel. She looked into the distance. At least most of the people she'd met.

Astrid picked up her bag and started off again, her curiosity nagging at her. As she continued to swim, she passed colorful coral forests, kelp forests, and sometimes just vast expanses of red or brown sand. Some stretches were silent in their lack of movement, but every now and then she would catch a glimpse of a bioluminescent creature above her or to the side. Their usually slow, squishy forms gave her the comfort of knowing she wasn't the only living thing in this expanse that seemed like it never ended.

She looked at the coordinate director over and over again. It seemed so close, yet so far.

The city emerged on the horizon. She couldn't tear her eyes away from it as she drew nearer. Velee spread before her, so unlike her own home. Colorful buildings twisted everywhere, no sharp lines and very few straight ones. They were much taller than Akaytan buildings. Dozens of them were temples scrawled with the names of gods she didn't recognize. Every structure was different, unlike Akayta. Even from this distance she could see masses of merpeople swimming by.

It all struck her as chaotic. There was no order, no one took the time to make sure that any of it complimented each other. It was a jumble and clash of colors and shapes that didn't fit together. It was especially hard on the eyes because all of the structures were extremely close to each other.

Her heart beat faster the closer she got. Her feelings were a mix of horror at what would be happening in a few weeks unless someone listened to her, and curiosity about how this new society would treat her.

With growing apprehension she swam into the city. *Which tribe is this? Do they still speak my language? What should I do?* Astrid felt almost overwhelmed. Here she was, getting bumped every which way. She turned, the crowd was much thicker than it ever was in Akayta. She wasn't used to this, and few even glanced at her. Those that did, didn't show surprise or disdain at her mark.

I'd better begin with the basics and find out where I am and try to figure out how their government works. Then I can get the information about the core to the necessary officials.

Astrid noticed that there were a lot of tiny fish with sharp teeth darting around. *Pest fish.* In Akayta, they were exterminated. It was rare to catch sight of one in the city, but here they were abundant. Masses of people swarmed on the wide path. People scattered as large transports barreled through, and vehicles zipped between them. It was hectic. The whole city was wild and chaotic.

At the side of the path, portable stands were set up, and each held something different. Grotesque figures, personal gods, rough fabrics, wild luna berries, and so much more. The colors and smells were utterly overwhelming in a way she'd never experienced before.

Merchants selling their wares in the middle of the city? That would never be allowed in Akayta. I might as well use it to my advantage. She swam up to the nearest stand, where a stocky, middle-aged merwoman sat busily peddling her creations.

"Excuse me, but could you tell me what city this is?" asked Astrid quietly.

The woman gave her a strange look. "You're in Velee, where else would you be?" Her language was very similar to Astrid's, but it had some quirks that were different from her own.

How do I find out about this city without seeming like I'm crazy? Astrid didn't know much about Velee besides its name and a little background.

She studied the woman's work-hardened face. Her eyes were intelligent. *I need someone I can trust.* Astrid looked around and felt alone. The street teemed with people, but in it all she felt hopelessly lost.

How was she supposed to warn them? Who should she warn? Were they ruled by a royal family also? Some of the people had marks, but the marks were all different kinds of things. Everything from twisting flowers all across an arm to words on a neck. And though the majority had these types of marks, not all of them did. Each person wore a cacophony of colors and scarves tied on their arms and heads rather randomly, from what Astrid could tell. They were so different from the neat, simple outfits of the Akaytans. Hopefully their attitudes would be different as well.

She looked back to the patiently waiting, gray-haired woman and held out her hand, deciding to take a leap. "I'm Astrid."

The woman shook her hand with a puzzled brow and said, "And my name is Delta."

Astrid squirmed uncomfortably, "May I have a word with you in private?"

"Yes…" Delta slowly got up and ushered her into a bright red house behind the stand. When they were inside, the confusion on Delta's face was evident. *How should I begin? I'm about to tell a perfect stranger why I'm here. But then again, it's all to save everyone.*

"I know that I don't know you or anything but there is something really important that everyone in this city needs to know. And I need some help." She paused for a moment trying to decipher the look on the woman's face. Delta stayed quiet.

Astrid continued, "I am from Akayta and…"

The woman's eyes widened in surprise, stopping Astrid. "Akayta?"

"Yes, and basically I discovered that in six weeks the core is going to explode."

Delta looked skeptical. "I'm sorry, but that's completely outlandish."

"It's true! Here, do you know about the melions? These are the results of an experiment I did," Astrid desperately thrust her notetablet with the results into the woman's hands. Delta nodded her head as she looked down at it. Every second that passed her eyes grew wider.

"You're right," she whispered, "our world is coming crashing down in six weeks." She looked up sharply. "I have a feeling that there is more to your story. Sit down and tell me."

Astrid did, telling her about the refusal to listen in Akayta and being completely clueless about Velee.

When she was done, Delta leaned back on the puffy chair thoughtfully, "Well, here in Velee we are a democracy, we are led by a leader called the high commander who proposes laws that the people vote on. You need to have a meeting with the high commander. General meetings are public, so others will be watching you as well."

"How do I get one of these meetings?" Astrid asked intently.

"It's simple," Delta answered. She got up and swam to a shelf where she pulled out a device that looked like a notetablet.

Her fingers tapped away for a few seconds then she looked up and said, "I've scheduled you to have a meeting with the high commander in three days. I'm sorry I couldn't get one sooner, but that was the first spot available."

Astrid's head spun as though she were in the middle of a storm. Her brain tried to go five different directions at once and was getting all muddled in the process.

"But I don't know…"

The woman put her fingers to Astrid's lips. "No buts. You can and will do it. This is important. It's not about you."

"Then why don't you do it?" Astrid asked in desperation.

"Because it is your testimony to give, not mine." She continued, "Come back in three days and I will take you there."

Astrid got up. "Thank you." Then she began to leave.

Delta sighed and asked gently, "Wait. Do you have a place to stay?"

Astrid hesitated.

Delta ushered her back in. "Come on. You can stay with me until it's time for your meeting.

Astrid smiled and almost cried. Here was a perfect stranger being kind to her.

CHAPTER FOUR

"Make yourself comfortable. I need to go close up my stand. I'll be back in half an hour." With that, Delta was out the door. Astrid sat awkwardly on the couch, not quite knowing what to do with herself. She felt like she should be doing something, but what was there to do? She wanted to look around a little bit, but that felt like a strange thing to do in Delta's house, even though she'd told Astrid to make herself comfortable. *I wonder if she lives alone.* Astrid got up and turned in a circle, making observations from where she hovered. The spacious living room opened straight into the dining room and kitchen. She sat down again. Before she knew it, her tiredness took over and she fell asleep.

She hadn't realized how tired she was until she finally stopped. A journey, a new culture, and a new acquaintance. Her mind swam as she went to sleep, telling her it wasn't polite to go to sleep on a stranger's couch, but she ignored that and drifted into a dream where words from an old book floated through her mind.

For four long, painful years the darkness was full and unsubtle. Truth was forgotten in almost everything, and hope was so scarce the freeday couldn't sing. I was fearful of so much, just like everyone else. I stole for food, and huddled up in terror during the blackouts, just like everyone else. But then I was called. I was meant to be someone new. I was meant to be different. A frightening thought to say the least. I was already barely surviving, why would I want to slim that chance even more?

But I had to. When the moment came and I was given the choice, there were only two options. To jump or to be pulled into the abyss. I chose to jump.

A sound entered Astrid's consciousness and began to pull her from her favorite passage of a book called *Freed.* She didn't want to leave her sleepy state and wake, so she tried to fall back into the dream. She had always loved that passage because she wished it was how she could be, but how?

If anyone in Akayta heard that wish, they would laugh at her. A lowly sixteen doing something worth praise? Unthinkable.

She felt a hand on her forehead and then on her fin. She moaned, turning her head the other direction. Delta's voice came through her fog. "Poor thing. She has a fever. Go get me a cold compress please, Alluvial."

Within minutes, Astrid felt a cold spot on her stomach.

The soothing voice continued, "That's the best place to bring the fever down because the tail holds most of the heat, but if you apply coldness on the tail itself, it causes clash sickness. She's been through a lot, Alluvial. I'm afraid that the worst might be yet to come. The least we can do is let her stay here for a few…"

Astrid didn't catch any more as she drifted off to sleep, but she was left with a feeling of gratefulness blanketing her mind.

She woke up groggily a few hours later, feeling much cooler and less tired. Sitting up, she remembered what had happened and where she was. Astrid heard a noise behind her as she sat up. She turned. It was Delta, who was in the kitchen making dinner. Getting up, she awkwardly faced her.

"Look, I'm so sorry I went to sleep and…"

"Why are you apologizing? No reason for that sort of thing. I hope you're feeling better."

Delta smiled slightly as she interrupted. She mixed some gostu spice into a bowl filled with a doughy, light blue substance.

"Take a seat," she said, motioning with her head to a stool at the dining table.

Astrid quietly swam over and sat down.

After a few minutes Delta spoke as she continued to prepare a meal. "Family? Friends? Hobbies? Tell me about yourself."

Astrid looked up from her hands in surprise. It was a rare occasion for someone to ask her about herself. "Well...I have one older sister who is living. That's all as far as family goes. And friends for that matter. She's the only person in Akayta who cares about me at all. Her name is Effie."

Delta paused and raised an eyebrow. "In *all* of Akayta? You have no other friends?"

Astrid blushed and looked down at the mark on her arm. "I used to have another one but he...disappeared. You see...in Akayta we have a caste system that ranks us by birth order. I am a sixteenth born. That's what this mark on my arm means. I'm pretty much at the bottom. People don't want to be friends with someone like me. It would damage their reputation. Besides, they think they're too good for me."

"Do *you* think they are too good for you?" asked Delta.

Astrid stuttered, "W-when I think about it, no, but that thought doesn't help the feeling in my heart that I'm stupid and forever shamed because of who I am."

"There is nothing that makes you less valuable than any one of them."

"But that's so hard to believe when everything and everyone around you is telling you that you're worthless!" replied Astrid desperately.

Delta continued mixing something in a bowl and turned the conversation in a new direction.

"What career are you planning to go into?"

"I'm not supposed to be going into *anything*— besides cleaning up their messes," Astrid said, exasperated with her situation. She sighed. "But I'm a scientist. I've been doing science experiments secretly. Actually, that's how I found out about the melions."

"I see. Your sister...what does she do?"

"Scientist. She's a firstborn."

"Yet you don't hate her?" Delta asked.

"Of course not. She's great," said Astrid, expressing more surprise at the suggestion than she truly felt. That was an uncomfortable undercurrent that she'd often quashed down. She refused to let jealousy have a permanent foothold in her heart, but sometimes she couldn't keep it from surfacing.

Delta smiled. "Well, that right there tells me you don't have the same prejudice against those people as they do against you."

Astrid looked down. She didn't want to admit it to herself, but in a way she did. She was angry with them for treating her and others like her so badly. They were wrong. They were oppressive. Yet she didn't stand up to them to tell them that it was wrong. She was afraid. And she was ashamed of that.

"What about you? Do you have any family?" Astrid asked.

"Yes. Actually, here comes my daughter right now."

From a hallway on the other side of the large area came a girl of about fifteen. She had a thin face and thoughtful light brown eyes to go along with her curly brown hair. The girl approached and smiled at Astrid.

"This is Alluvial," said Delta.

The girl waved.

"Hi," replied Astrid with a sincere smile.

"It's nice to meet you," she replied quietly.

Astrid grinned.

Three days passed and the dreaded day arrived. Astrid had to address the Veleens and tell them about the melions. She worked all morning uselessly trying to come up with ideas on how to start the speech.

Astrid looked up as she heard a small creaking noise. Delta was coming in. That meant it was time to leave.

"Are you ready?" she asked.

"Not really…" Astrid replied unsurely.

"You'll do fine," Delta said in a way that sounded like a command. There was no room for argument. "Astrid, I have to warn you that Veleens generally don't have a long attention span," she hesitated, "and they can be very cruel."

She swallowed and replied, "What choice do I have? And…thank you for being so kind to me."

Delta nodded and smiled.

Astrid stood awkwardly waiting for Delta to tell her what to do.

Delta motioned with her head toward the door, "Well…"

"Oh…" she whispered and then swam through the door back out into the sunshine.

Delta followed.

Alluvial stood in the doorway as they exited, flashing her bright smile. "Good day, Astrid. Good luck!"

Astrid smiled. "Hope to see you soon.'

With that Delta took the lead and Astrid followed. She attempted to steel herself. Truth be told, she had no idea what the day would bring. Her entire future was in a state of flux. Not even knowing what the evening would hold for her brought with it a kind of exhilaration and trepidation she had never known.

The city was incredibly bustling. People pushed past her every time she tried to make an inch of headway. But somehow, Astrid kept up with Delta and finally made it to where the meeting would take place. She struggled, trying to look over all the moving heads and see the podium better.

Delta grabbed her hand and pulled her through the swarming mass. When they got to the front Astrid took it all in. There was a wooden podium that stood about five feet above the crowd. On either side of it large screens glowed, comically mismatched with the worn wooden stand. She smirked. *Hodge-podge, just like the rest of this city.* They read, "The Commander Meeting will begin in one minute."

"Come on. You have to get up there." Delta said, giving Astrid a small push.

She turned back to the worn woman with a pleading gaze, "Please do this for me. I can't." Her stomach churned in dread. "You have to understand, I'm not a public speaker."

"This is not about being good speaker. It's about the message. Now go."

Astrid grew pale as she swam up and took one of the two black chairs facing the crowd. The countdown was now at five seconds. Then a tinny piece of music played over a sound system as a merman came out onto the stage. His demeanor was self-righteous as he waved to the crowd dotingly. Surprisingly, he didn't have the presence or authoritative posture she would have expected. The middle-aged man had white hair, and pomp etched into the lines of his face. *I can't believe this is the high commander.*

He sat down and, after grinning for a few minutes and waving to the adoring people, he finally turned to Astrid and handed her a mic patch. She took the small orange square and attached it to her arm with trembling fingers.

The merman then turned to the crowd and his voice pounded through the speakers.

"Today our good Astrid has scheduled a meeting. Let us hear what she has to say, as is the custom in our ancient and orderly democracy!" Then he turned and motioned for her to begin.

Astrid faced the crowd. She felt dizzy as silence surrounded her. *How do I even start?*

She took a deep breath. "I...I have some information that is...very important to you all."

As she looked at the sea of faces, they started to blend together in an endless muddle.

Then one face stood out to her. A young man. His cutting green eyes pierced hers, and his jaw was set intensely. Unruly black hair waved in the water. His expression was the epitome of defiance, and he looked maybe eighteen or nineteen. She couldn't tear her gaze from his face. There was something about him that kept her staring. He felt powerful...magnetic.

And he kept staring at her. His face unflinching. His gaze iron. She couldn't read his expression.

Rune? My Rune. But that was impossible.

"Miss Astrid?" came the comatose voice of the high commander.

She looked up and remembered where she was. She took a deep breath as she tried to recover her train of thought.

"Umm...I have data...that," she took a deep breath to calm herself, "that shows that the cadence of the melions are off and in less than six weeks the core will explode."

A silence hung in the air for several seconds. Astrid felt uncomfortable. It was a silence of disbelief, not panic.

Finally a woman near the front shouted, "You're crazy!"

Agreement ran through the crowd.

"But wait, I have the data right here!" she shouted with desperation.

"I bet it's falsified!" yelled someone else.

"But…" She felt weak, losing any words she might've had left.

Jeering began.

Cries of, "Get her off the stage!" and, "Throw her in a mental cell!" rose into the water.

No one believes me here. It's just as bad as Akayta. Panic consumed her.

She was used to being quiet— not because she couldn't speak, but because that was what people expected of her. Now she was trying to speak up, but it felt like her voice was hitting a brick wall.

The high commander turned to her with a smirk and said over the speakers, "Well, the people have decided their opinion of you and now they shall decide your fate as well, as is the custom of our ancient and orderly democracy."

The crowd broke into a cheer and suddenly merpeople were swarming about Astrid, pulling at her, yanking her down. *This isn't democracy. This is anarchy!* Hands snatched at her arms and tail. She couldn't see anything as she was pinched and pricked everywhere, and merpeople were surrounding her.

"Stop! Stop!" she screamed.

An especially strong grip landed on her wrists and pulled. *I'm going to die,* she realized with a shock. She was being pricked by many small, needled devices. Astrid didn't know what they were, but she guessed whatever they did probably wasn't meant to be helpful. Someone still had a strong grip on her wrists. Astrid flung her arms around in an attempt to shake it loose. Suddenly, she was pulled deeper into the crowd.

She was still being attacked, but less and less. Confusion arose behind her, where she'd been seconds before. It was murky. She caught a whiff of the distinct smell. *It has to be mind gas.*

She realized the pair of hands were still gripping her wrists. As one let go and began to pull her through the crowd, she looked up to meet their owner. Astrid couldn't see his face at first as the fled the mob. She tried to free herself until the realization dawned on her, *Someone's rescuing me.*

Screams filled the water now and people pushed past Astrid, not even giving her a second glance. She saw a particularly crowded section of the city looming. The stranger made several abrupt turns, the final one into a dark, abandoned alley hidden from the view of the market. The brick walls were dotted with algae and dirt, but their cool sturdiness felt protective. She immediately peeled off the mic patch and tore it into a dozen pieces, scattering it over the ocean floor.

Then her rescuer turned to face her. His eyes cut straight to her immediately and she gasped. It was the same boy she'd seen in the crowd.

He quickly averted his eyes. His expression was very...unsettled? Confused? He sighed in disbelief as he looked into the watery sky and ran his hand through his hair in potent dismay. Astrid struggled inside herself. *Why did this person just rescue me and why is he acting so frustrated? I didn't ask him to do that.* Astrid looked down at her hands and played with them nervously.

After a few seconds she looked back up and said, "Thanks for saving me. I'm Astrid."

He glanced back at her again with a look of near panic...and yet, something more.

"I know."

His answer was short, but there were so many emotions injected into it.

"How did you know my...Oh yeah, the high commander introduced me to the crowd." Why was he so upset? She examined him more closely. He wore a shiny dark red shirt with full length sleeves and his tail was a deep shade of blue she couldn't stop staring at. He looked strikingly like an older Rune. She would have thought it was him, except for the fact that she didn't want to get her hopes up and look like an idiot in the process. But...his face had Rune written all over it. She knew those features oh so very well. The resemblance felt like a knife through her heart, so she glanced away. *I'm imagining things because this person looks like him. I'm just tricking myself now. Am I really that desperate? Or maybe I'm just going crazy,* she thought sarcastically.

Pulling her arms around herself she asked, "How about you? What's your name?"

He paused for a moment before answering. "Mist. My name is Mist."

"You remind me of someone I used to know."

"Sorry, but I've never met you."

Astrid paused and then sighed, *It's just my imagination running away with me.*

"Listen, Astrid, I believe you and I know these people are...hard to deal with. They were warned, so your job is done. I know a safe place where you can stay. I'll take you there. You might want to put your head down and hide your face so we can avoid any more outbursts from bloodthirsty Veleens," he stated kindly before turning and starting to swim away. His calm, controlled voice sent a wave of comfort through her.

She began to follow, but he stopped abruptly and turned back around. "I forgot. Please sit down for just a second."

Astrid looked at him unsurely as she sat down against the wall. She didn't know what to make of this boy. He came closer and knelt down beside her.

"They hurt you," he said quietly.

She hadn't noticed until that moment but there were six pricks on her right arm. Thin trickles of thick red Akaytan blood flowed out into the water and drifted down to the floor of the alley without dispersing.

"It's no big deal," she replied.

Mist didn't reply, he just took a medical wipe packet out of a pocket and began to wipe her arm down. The little dots began to sting as pressure was applied.

"What were they pricking me with?"

Mist didn't answer. After a few seconds he was done and stood up again.

"I need to get you to the Complex," he said under his breath, almost to himself.

The he turned to her, "We need to get going. Come on." His tone was urgent.

Confusion swirled through her mind. She was trying to process the whole situation, but so much didn't make sense.

He took her hand and helped her up. She expected him to let go, but he didn't. He just turned, his rough hand gripping hers.

"Remember, keep your head down," Mist said gently as they plunged into the noisy mass of people in the market.

Astrid's heart sped up as they swam straight through the crowd that wanted to kill her only minutes ago.

They neared the edge of town. There were now only a few individuals here and there, which wasn't necessarily a good thing. She felt exposed. As they passed by the colorful buildings, Astrid's breathing sped up. Everything began to tilt. *What's happening?* She could feel herself starting to fall.

"Mist!" she called as her body filled with a dull sense of pain.

He turned, his hand slipping from hers as she fell. The moment felt as though it were in slow motion. Her mind, which was beginning to cloud with delirium, watched her hand slide from his. It sent a wave of pain through her as she felt like it had happened before, when Rune had been pulled from her life.

"Not yet, Astrid, not yet," Mist whispered as he scooped her up. She was conscious, but every thought felt clouded and pain flowed through her. She groaned. Astrid examined Mist's face. He didn't looked surprised at all as he swam on, but he was intense and had an air of urgency.

"What's the matter with me?" she managed to ask.

"They poisoned you," he said, pointing to the pricks. "I know a place where you'll be safe and can get treated."

His presence was powerful, and his jaw set with determination bordering on panic. He looked so much like Rune...but this was a perfect stranger. Why would he care about her?

"Why?" she voiced her thoughts almost without realizing it. She felt herself heating up and things were becoming cloudy. *Delirious. I'm becoming...delirious.*

Mist stopped in his tracks and looked down into her face, "What?"

He resumed swimming as she answered, her eyes fluttering open, then closing again, "Why're you doing...this? Helping me? In my experience...people are more prone to look down on you because they want to feel good about themselves...they have to have a class of people who they can despise. There've only been...two or three people in my entire life who've cared about me at all...who thought I...am worth something...but maybe everyone's right. I'm only one of so many...how important can I be? If I died today only one person would mourn me...then I'd be forgotten forever...The other person is long gone...I hope in my heart that he escaped...but I know that's just wishful thinking. My hope left with him..." in her delirium, she poured out her heart to him.

His expression was unchanging as he continued on, though his eyes betrayed the storm raging within him. "You must have been very unknowing to go up there and tell the Veleens that the core is going to explode. They are a volatile people. For the most part they despise logic and enjoy bloodshed, and you just accidently gave them a new target. Whatever the case, I decided to save you."

Astrid heard the answer, but the ability to process wasn't available to her. She faded in and out of consciousness.

"We're almost there."

She heard Mist's voice, then her face started tingling. Blackness viciously and silently closed in around her.

CHAPTER FIVE

Rune perched across from her on a rock outcropping. He smiled as they sat silently staring at the massive dome of the cave. Rune seemed to have an affinity for caves. They'd been friends for a while, and in that time he'd shown her quite a few. I think they make him feel safe, *she thought.*

Rune looked at her with a grin and asked, "What are you smiling about?"

"I was just thinking what a...unique person you are."

"Bad or good?" he asked with a laugh.

"Let's see, you're confident and rather defiant, you don't see any limits when there are nothing but limits for us, and...you're friends with me," she listed out on her fingers. "That last one sounded more like a reason when it was in my head than when I actually said it. I think those are all good things."

"Being friends with you counts as something unique...strange?" he asked, raising his eyebrows.

She looked down. *"There is only one other person who wants to be my friend, and she's my sister."*

Rune got up from where he'd been sitting across from her and slid down beside her against the cold, calming grey stone.

"You're a very special person, and I'm honored to be your friend. People don't see your value— not because it isn't there, but because they've been raised in a mindset where red-and-blacks are two-dimensional characters who can't think for themselves and aren't worth the time of day. You and I both know how untrue it is, even if it still hurts."

"I know," she whispered. They rarely discussed the issue, even though it permeated every thought and action.

"It frustrates me how everyone believes in the Sirof just to keep us in bondage," he remarked.

Astrid stared at him for a moment before quietly asking, *"Do you think there's anything else after we die?"*

"Not the Afterlife. The Sirof were never real, and that wasn't either. But I can't help thinking there must be something else."

"Like what?"

He sighed. *"I don't know what to think. I'm lost when it comes to philosophy, so I never look too closely. I'm deathly afraid of it, Astrid. Look at what religion has done in Akayta.*

"Anyway, I just try to do my best to have good character and leave it at that."

Astrid paused for a moment. "Someday I hope to find the answer to those questions. It's mind-boggling how much we don't know about the universe, how much we don't know about our own lives," she replied, pulling her fin up to rest her chin on it.

Rune leaned his head against the wall and looked up at the ceiling. After a moment he spoke, relieving the tension of the heavy conversation. "Alright, your turn...you're unique because you're...smart but don't always show it. You're strong, though someone watching on the street might not see it immediately. You love science, it's an art to you. And you have a way of being there for people when they need you."

Astrid laughed. "Now you're describing yourself."

He smiled. "You're a beautiful person. That's why I like you."

"Is that supposed to be a compliment?"

He glanced back at her with a twinkle in his eye. "I meant a beautiful personality, but you are stunningly beautiful you know."

She just laughed.

Breath rushed into her lungs and she grasped for it desperately— water had been in absence, it must have been. She needed it so badly, so badly.

Her breath wavered as her lungs burned, trying to...needing to...suck in more, but also needing to breathe out. Her body shuddered as cold suddenly rushed over her and her eyes flew open. The dream only echoed for a second in her mind before she woke up fully. She tried to take in everything all at once. A black room filled with white instruments. She was lying in a white, soft bed and the lights were dim. Two merpeople watched her. They were both women.

One looked young. Her cheeks were full, her heart-shaped face smiling as her wide frame hovered in excitement.

She leaned over to the other woman, a brunette, and whispered, "She's awake."

Their hair was pinned up in tight buns and they wore black coats. The woman with the heart-shaped face had her sleeves rolled up. And on her arm just below her shoulder was a black and red symbol.

Astrid gasped. *Nine. She's a nine! Am I back in Akayta? No, they wouldn't be taking care of me.* Red-and-blacks were only allowed to have an hour of hospital time a year for minor injuries like scrapes, unless they were royalty. Besides, Akaytan hospitals weren't painted black. *Where am I?*

Her experience with the Veleens and Mist flashed through her head. She groaned as her memory cleared and she remembered her delirious conversation with him. She'd told him some of her innermost feelings, and that made her vulnerable. *He said he was taking me somewhere safe, but where is here? And where is Mist?* She tried to focus and ignore the nausea as she slowly sat up. The two women just floated patiently as they watched her. Their gazes were disconcerting. Astrid stared into the women's eyes as the silence became unbearable. She had to say something to avert the pressure.

She blurted out the first thing that came to mind, "Where is Mist?"

They looked at each other in shock.

"Mist!" one exclaimed.

She turned back to Astrid, "What do you know about Mist?"

Why do they seem so surprised? Mist brought me here, so they shouldn't be surprised that I would mention him. I'd better be careful how I answer. Something is strange about this whole thing.

Astrid's voice cracked slightly from disuse as she replied, "I just know he brought me here and I was curious as to where he is."

"He brought you here!" gasped the woman with the heart-shaped face, whose blonde hair was just starting to come out of her bun.

Astrid ignored the exclamation. Panic was starting to build in her stomach. She had to know where she was to regain some control or at least some understanding of her circumstances.

"Where am I and what happened?" she asked.

The blonde woman responded, "We found you lying right outside of the complex and quickly found that you'd been poisoned, so we took care of you. It's been two days now. You are in the Star tribe."

Astrid wrinkled her brow, "The Star tribe? But there are only three tribes. Velee, Fillerra, and Akayta. And you, you have the mark of someone born in Akayta."

The other woman answered, "We will let the guider decide what he wishes to tell you. I will go alert him of your consciousness and he will come as soon as he can."

With that she abruptly exited the room, leaving the blonde woman behind. There was a pleasant air about her.

She gazed at Astrid steadily and finally held out her hand, "I'm Adamaris. You can call me Ris. What's your name?"

Astrid hesitantly shook Ris's hand, "Astrid. How-how long have you been here?"

"I've lived here for two years. I ran away from Akayta when I was fourteen." Ris twisted her hands together nervously.

Unpleasant memories of a lifetime of abuse rushed through Astrid's mind, and she realized that the girl before her must have experienced the same thing.

"You're sixteen years old? So am I. Actually, I'm about to turn seventeen," said Astrid awkwardly.

Ris suddenly sat down and took Astrid's hands in her own, "It's okay! Don't worry, it's great here. Not perfect, but so much better than Akayta. People won't despise you anymore You'll see that you're worth something. Trust me. I know."

Astrid smiled as a tear floated out of her eye. She felt an instant connection with this girl. They understood each other.

It was only a minute before Astrid heard a whoosh and the other woman entered once again. Someone trailed behind her. Astrid waited for the person to come into the light. When he did, her heart fell into her stomach.

It was Mist, but it wasn't...he looked almost exactly like Mist. Only a few, small details seemed different. His nose was slightly more rounded and his hair was a little longer. There was also a different type of air about him...a frighteningly intense air...one that Astrid didn't know how to read. *Who is he?* He stared her down. Frozen, his deep green eyes seemed to be analyzing her very soul.

Astrid was at a loss as to how to start a conversation. Her other questions seemed void in comparison to his striking resemblance to Mist and...Rune for that matter. His face kept flashing through her mind. It couldn't be coincidence that this man, Mist, and Rune all looked so similar. She also wondered at the shock of Ris and the other woman at hearing the name Mist.

The man's hands were clasped behind his back. His attitude was confident and self-assured. He turned his head slightly, but kept his eyes on Astrid.

The two women went to monitors on the other side of the room, Ris giving Astrid a reassuring glance before she turned away.

As they stared at each other, it felt like a stalemate, neither wishing to speak first. Finally he broke the silence.

"I heard that Mist brought you here."

"Yes..."

"I'm sure you have a great deal of curiosity, so I'll explain." He sat down opposite her. His focus on her was so sharp, it was almost disconcerting. "I don't know exactly where to begin. Well, you met Mist." A long pause followed. Heavy water seemed to pervade the space between every word. "He's my twin brother. I'll tell you more about him in a minute, but first I have to tell you

who I am. I'm Rune, Astrid. It's me."
Desperation filled his voice and face.

Astrid clutched the sheets so hard she felt like her fingers would break. She closed her eyes and tried to breathe evenly. *Rune. It's Rune.* A volley of emotions slammed into her chest as she tried to process it. She opened her eyes and saw him from a new perspective. That of a hope fulfilled.

"Rune?" she whispered.
He just smiled. The smile was so genuine it made her grin. Then something hit her.

"Wait...you have a twin brother?"
He grimaced, "Unfortunately."
She was silent, waiting for him to continue.
He sighed, "I'll start from the beginning. Mist and I endured the harshness of being red-and-blacks together." His eyes gained a far off look, "We helped each other, but eventually we both grew restless. Mist decided to leave first and I decided to follow a couple of years later. We found each other hiding on the outskirts of Velee and reconnected. It turned out that Mist had been committing thefts here and there, but never truly made himself known. I, on the other hand, had this strong desire to help people that are outcasts, like us. Here in my tribe we have many people who are considered outcasts by their societies, but have committed no wrong. Anyway, I decided as I met more and more people like me

that we needed a refuge. A place where we can all belong. So I founded a new tribe. I tried to convince Mist to join me, but he is a coward." His eyes darkened in a way that made Astrid's heart miss a beat.

Something had changed in Rune over the past two years. *I suppose I've changed as well.*

Rune continued, "He was afraid that we'd be attacked by the other tribes. Velee especially. When the Veleens dub someone as an outcast, they're quite vicious about persecuting them. I've only seen him once since then, but there are rumors about his exploits as a criminal. He's bad news, Astrid."

Many thoughts swirled through her head, *Why was Mist so kind to me? Why did he bring me here? How did I never meet him in Akayta?* A strange feeling of intrigue ran through her. *I wish I could talk to him more. I'll probably never see him again.*

Astrid just didn't know how to respond. She stuttered over several syllables, but ended up in silence.

His eyes softened as he looked at her, "I know this is all new to you, Astrid, but you're home. This is where I belong, and this is where you belong also."

There was something about this whole, exhilarating situation that made Astrid's heart race. It was plunging, but at the same time rising.

She was in complete control of her decisions at this moment. And that had *never* happened before. If she got herself in trouble it would be her fault, but she had the opportunity to make her own choices.

No more being shackled by the system. No more of Effie's comforting protection. The knife cut both ways.

CHAPTER SIX

No more need for fear. Despite the realization, the fear of no friends— no people she could truly trust— gnawed at her heart still. Maybe you can make a friend instantly, but that doesn't mean you trust them. Trust takes time, no matter the circumstances.

Astrid was suddenly jolted out of her thoughts when Rune stood up and said, "You must be hungry and tired. After all, you were just saved from deadly Veleen poison. I'll let you rest. We can talk more later."

He turned to leave. She held out her hand and asked the question at the forefront of her mind, "Why did Mist care for me if he is so intent on his own safety? He carried me almost the entire way after rescuing me from a mob of bloodthirsty merpeople."

Rune froze and slowly turned, "Mist only helps people if it is to his advantage. That means that you have something of value that he wants. Avoid him."

He was out of the room before she could reply.

Silence fell uncomfortably. Questions battered her thoughts in an unending cycle. She turned to Ris.

"Would you be terribly annoyed if I asked a few questions? To tell the truth I feel pretty lost right now."

Ris turned from her post and smiled hesitantly, "I'm not supposed to tell you anything about our complex until Rune gives official approval...but I know him and I can tell that he's going to. I'll start with the basics."

"You already know that you're in the Star tribe. There are only about five thousand of us. As he told you, we're a group of people that are considered outcasts. We live together, work together, and support each other. We have operatives in all the tribes who are working toward making them more friendly toward people like us. Rune has an ultimate plan that he's working toward to completely eliminate prejudice and violence from the tribes, but most of us don't have all the details yet. Pieces are falling into place every day. We're just waiting for the time when he gives each of us an assignment, then we'll follow it. Eventually we'll all get them he says. So... you know him?" she asked curiously.

Astrid took a deep breath. She wanted to believe in this utopia led by a boy who used to be her closest friend, but it seemed too good to be true. *Maybe that's just because all my life people have been cruel to me. I've almost stopped believing that good exists. I need to learn trust, and this is the place to do it. Of all things, it's led by my friend.*

"Um...yeah. When he still lived in Akayta we were good friends. Then he disappeared and...I didn't know what happened to him until now."

She stared down at her hands. He hadn't told her he was going to leave. He'd just left. The last thing he'd told her was to never let her mark restrict her. She never thought she'd see him again, but here he was.

And then there was Mist. She'd seen so many things and met so many new people the last few days that she felt like the entire world was new. But Astrid wasn't sure if she liked this new world.

She slept for several days on and off. On the third morning she woke up to Ris shaking her shoulder.

"You're ready to go now," she said kindly.

She sat up groggily, even in her sleep the words, "go now" caught her attention. She began to panic. Where would she go? She couldn't go back to Akayta and the Veleens would tear her apart. As she finally became completely awake, she realized that Ris just meant she was healed.

"Am I allowed to stay?" she asked hesitantly.

This world was so fresh. She felt lost. *The only person I can depend on is myself. I don't have Effie anymore.*

"Actually, Rune wants to talk to you again. I wouldn't worry though. We've only ever turned one person away," she replied reassuringly.

"Who did you turn away?" the question popped out before Astrid had time to think about it.

Ris's ice blue tail squirmed. She looked uncomfortable, like maybe she shouldn't answer, but she did anyway, "Mist. He came just a few months ago and asked Rune to let him in. Rune said he didn't qualify as an outcast anymore and that he wouldn't risk our safety for that of a criminal. I'd suggest not talking about it with anyone here. It's kind of a...sensitive topic since he's someone so close to Rune."

Astrid nodded with shock. *Why would Mist want into a tribe that he originally refused to join? Maybe he's on the run. Rune said he'd been committing thefts. What about Mist's strange reaction to me?*

She just couldn't forget the look on his face as she spilled her heart out to him. Curiosity nagged at her, making her want to understand him. She wanted to know him better, despite herself.

"Oh, yes. Here. I've some clothes you can change into," Ris said, turning away then picking up and giving Astrid a bundle of simple black clothes with a metallic look. It was the Star uniform.

"I'll leave you to change, then I'll take you to Rune."

Astrid nodded in understanding. After she changed, she wandered out the door hesitantly. Ris was waiting there, her full cheeks highlighting her smile.

"Come on."

Astrid followed her down colorful halls decorated with all kinds of art. Everything from murals to mounted statues. They were surrounded by doors in the twisty hall. Eventually they came to a door labeled, "The Guider." Ris stopped and knocked. A voice called, "Enter." The door opened automatically.

"You'll do fine," Ris whispered encouragingly before she turned and swam away, leaving Astrid at the door.

She timidly entered. Even if this was someone she used to know, she didn't feel like she knew him anymore. The room was round and cream-colored. Opposite the door was a curved blue desk. Rune sat behind it, reading something on a tablet. His magnetic eyes moved upwards when the automatic doors closed behind her. He sat back in his chair, expression unreadable.

"Take a seat," he said, gesturing to a comfortable chair.

She did as her heart rose into her throat and she studied her friend. He seemed so different. They'd been apart so long that she didn't feel comfortable around him anymore. Hopefully that would change. He'd been her closest friend. He'd been so much more than that...they had shared trials and their deepest feelings. He was like a part of her. Then why was she so uneasy? It would take time to remember that bond.

He watched her for a moment before saying, "Of course you can stay, Astrid. Ris told me that she explained to you about us. Normally it take a long time for someone to earn my trust enough to be assigned to a mission. But I know you, and I trust you. So you will be given a mission very soon. Once your assignment is chosen, you'll go through a small amount of training to prepare you for your particular job."

Astrid was shocked. *I can't go on missions! I...I'm not right for that type of thing..I can't...I just can't do it!*

"But I'd mess something up!" she exclaimed.

Rune smiled slightly. "I know you. You can't see it, but you're meant for greatness. There is something different about you from all other red-and-blacks I've seen. You hide behind a mask of being afraid and incompetent, because you know that anything else would seem out of place for a sixteen. But if you let that mask go, you're just as confident as anyone else out there. You dare to do what's right. I heard about what happened in Velee. If you don't call that brave, I don't know what you call it."

Astrid blushed. *Mist called it "unknowing,"* she remembered, his words coming back to her mind. Her heart pounded as she felt like she was holding back millions of emotions. The description he'd just given of her didn't sound right. Maybe he thought that she was brave, but she was scared. Scared to be something people would reject.

Astrid knew, though, that there was a small wisp of truth in what he was saying. If something needed to be done to help someone, if it came down to it, she would act— even if she was uncomfortable. She took a deep breath.

Everything rushed at her, trying to be overwhelming. *It doesn't have to be. It'll be fine.*

"I need you to explain to me about the core. That might require making some major changes to our plan," he said.

"Well, the melions' cadence has gotten off-kilter. They're going to explode in less than six weeks."

He looked shocked for a moment, but then his gaze became thoughtful.

"Is there any way we could do something to fix it?"

"I doubt it. The melions are tiny particles deep within the core. It would take forever to isolate them and figure out how to stabilize them. I think the only solution is evacuation."

Rune's mouth twisted into a grim line as he crossed his arms. "I'll have to think about this."

After a moment, his face brightened slightly. "I'm sure everything will be fine. Now that we have business out of the way, I want to just talk with you. I haven't seen you in ages."

Astrid laughed, which surprised her. There were few times in her life when she actually laughed. And Rune was the cause of most of them.

"I don't know what to talk about. I haven't been doing anything extraordinarily interesting."

"Well, then let's talk about how you've been feeling. How are you, for real?" he asked, his eyes piercing hers.

She sobered. She barely let herself experience her feelings, she wasn't about to begin spewing them off to someone else. *Except I used to talk about them with Rune all the time.* She looked into the familiar green eyes. *Why do I keep thinking of him like he's a complete stranger? Yes, we've been apart for long time, but he remembers...and I remember what we went through together. I know him. I should trust him. He's still the same person. Still...I'm not ready to talk about my emotions.*

"Well...you know. I think you're the one we should talk about. Look at all you've been doing! When am I going to get a tour?" she smiled.

"How about now?"

"Alright."

His smile wasn't a grin, in fact, she hadn't seen him grin yet, which was one of the things she remembered about Rune. The Rune in front of her had a small smile, but it held a silent confidence instead of jocularity. Their time apart had taken its toll on him. He got up and led her down the halls. They were outside in a few minutes.

Astrid was amazed at what she saw. It wasn't necessarily the architecture or size of buildings that made it astonishing, it was what they stood for. Mermaids and mermen swam about smiling and talking. There was a great sense of camaraderie. She saw everything from nineteens to people with no markings at all, but they were all talking to each other. No one thought they were better than everyone else. It seemed like heaven to her. There weren't any of the rough, "I don't care about you" attitudes she'd seen in Velee, and there wasn't any of the disdain she'd seen in Akayta. *This is truly incredible.* The world seemed to be opening up. It was like she'd had a dark, stifling case enclosing her all her life, and a hole had just been cut in it, letting fresh, clean breezes sweep around her.

As for the buildings, they were glossy, gently curving structures, many of which were a vibrant blue. Surrounding the entire area was a tall, solid, white dome. *The complex. Mist said the complex. Ah! Why do I keep thinking about Mist?*

A voice interrupted her thoughts, "What do you think?"

She turned to Rune with a smile. "It's more than I could ever imagine. Amazing."

His eyes softened as he took her hand. "You're amazing, and I'm glad to have you back."

CHAPTER SEVEN

Astrid was with Rune as silent tears floated from his face. She sat by him quietly. That was all she could do as they rocked back and forth together.

"She's gone. My mother's gone, Astrid." His tear-filled eyes held her own for a moment before he looked back down at the ground.

Tears began falling down her own cheeks. Ellidah was a strong force in his life and in Astrid's for that matter. She'd never put up with the notion that red-and-blacks were inferior. Though he didn't say it, the double digit district loomed over Rune's future.

He gazed back up at her. "That's the last of my family. There's no one else."

Astrid reached over and took his hand.

She didn't tell him that things would get better, she didn't tell him that it was okay. She was just there for him, there to share his pain. As she put her arm around his shoulders, she was there for him as he had always been for her.

As Astrid woke up, the dream left a pang of sorrow in her heart. Memories like that would never be erased.

She sat at a table in the large, maroon-colored cafeteria of the complex three days later. Ris sat across from her saying something every now and then, but Astrid wasn't really trying to carry on a conversation. She wore one of the black shirts with mid-length sleeves that many wore. It was the official uniform, but most preferred to wear their own clothing as a form of expression. As for her, she felt like an automaton, missing that sense of individual identity. The outfit felt safe because she knew what it stood for. She hadn't brought extra clothes with her when she'd fled Akayta anyways.

Her eyes wandered over the surrounding faces, then stopped at one that sent shivers down her spine. In the young crowd, an old man stood out. He had a scraggly grey beard and eyes that held malice and deviance.

Ris saw where she was looking and leaned forward, her eyes flashing with fear. "His name is Cog. Avoid him," she whispered.

"Why?" Astrid asked.

Ris just gave a small shake of her head and glanced down at her food.

There was an awkward pause, but Astrid's mind moved on from the menacing man and turned to a new topic.

"Have you been on a mission yet, Ris?"

Ris got that uncomfortable look on her face again. Astrid was starting to recognize it.

"You have a knack for asking about things that are supposed to be under the radar," she said, shaking her head. She lowered her voice, "Here, missions are pretty...secretive. We don't talk about our missions or ask others about theirs. I will tell you though that, yes, I've been on one mission. There are different types of missions, but we only know about the types that we're assigned to."

"Why is it so secretive when everyone here knows the goal you're working toward?"

"The main point of our system is to avoid giving the plan away. If someone is caught, they can't tell what they don't know. No matter how much they might want to. Say they were tortured. The damage to us as a community would still be minimal

Astrid nodded, but to her it didn't make much sense. *It smells too much of deception. It would be more likely to inspire loyalty and unity if everyone knew the plan. But this is Rune I'm talking about. He'd never do anything underhanded, and in a way I guess it does make sense. I just don't agree with it.* Practically, she understood. But it seemed so rife with the potential for corruption. She put away her misgivings.

She'd spent the last few days with Rune, thinking, talking, and relaxing. She hadn't seen Ris since the hospital. But that morning Ris saw her sitting alone, and joined her. Another question popped up.

"What do you spend your days doing?"

In Akayta there were theaters, art houses, and a variety of other recreational buildings. Even though she'd never been able to enter them because of her status as a sixteenth child, she'd sat outside of them many, many times wondering what they were like inside.

"Well, we all have jobs. I've had the last few days off. I'm surprised you haven't been assigned one yet. That makes me think that you'll get a mission soon. When we're not working...we do have a special place we go," her eyes began to twinkle, and her dimples showed. "Oh, It's so much fun, Astrid! Much more fun than I think even the Akaytan recreational places would be. Do you want me to show it to you after we finish eating?"

Astrid smiled, "Definitely." She looked down at the heavy lumps of green olan on her plate. She'd always loved olan.

A restlessness occupied her body. In the back of her mind, a clock of doom seemed to be ticking down. Rune hadn't mentioned anything about the core since the first day she'd been well. *I told the Akaytans and the Veleens. Both rejected my message and tried to imprison or kill me. I gave them warning, so why do I feel like my job isn't done? Like I need to try again? The reaction is not going to change. What about the Fillerra though? I haven't heard anyone mention them. They need to be told.*

"Where are the Fillerra?" she asked abruptly, interrupting the silence.

Ris became solemn. "You don't know? I guess you wouldn't since you just came from Akayta."

"Know what?"

"The Fillerra were torn apart by a civil war a couple of years ago. They managed to wipe out everyone in the tribe. Well, almost everyone. Only one person escaped. Actually, she's sitting right over there," Adamaris replied, pointing to a serious-looking girl sitting at a table in the corner.

She was all alone. Something sad burned in her dark blue eyes. Her black hair hung around her face in thick waterfalls. Her indigo tail gave her an air of solemn beauty. Astrid's heart went out to her. At that moment she realized that everyone here had a backstory. A tale as to how they'd become outcasts, how they'd come to join the Star Tribe. All of them held wisps of the pain of rejection in their souls. All of them had sadness that they'd been forced to endure for years.

And we all have a fresh start.

"What's her name?" Astrid asked.

"Honor."

Astrid got up and began to swim toward her.

"I wouldn't recommend asking her about it...it's kind of a touchy topic."

Astrid turned her head back toward Ris as she kept swimming. "I wasn't planning on it."

Ris followed hesitantly.

When they reached the table, Honor peered up at them, not smiling.

"My name is Astrid," she said, holding out her hand.

Honor looked at it dubiously before shaking it. "Yes…"

"Well…I'm new and I wanted to meet some people and you...look like someone good to meet."

Honor looked back down at the book she'd been reading. "If you want to know about Fillerra, forget it. It's dead, and as far as I'm concerned the memory is dead also. Just leave me alone."

Astrid sat down. She could tell that what Honor said wasn't true. The memory still lived within her. It haunted her every day, every hour, and every minute. That much could be seen in her eyes. She was still dealing with her grief.

A current of discomfort ran through her. She'd never really tried to make friends in Akayta, and figured it would take some kind of guts. So she took a deep breath and decided to make friends with Honor. She felt like she understood her in a strange way. Even here, this girl seemed lonely. She needed a friend, and likewise, Astrid wanted to forge new relationships.

"No, that's not why I came over here."

"Oh, really? Why then? That's the only reason anyone ever wants to talk to me."

"I know what it's like to be alone, and I don't like to see anyone else alone."

Honor gave a harrumph, "You are new. *Everyone* here knows what it's like to be alone. I'm the outcast of the outcasts. I prefer it this way," she replied sarcastically. Her eyes returned to her book.

"No, you don't. I can see it in your eyes."

Honor slammed her book shut. "Would you just give up?"

Getting up, Astrid blushed a deep shade of red. Embarrassment overwhelmed her as she began to swim away. *Why would I even try that. Ugh!*

A deep sigh was issued, "Wait."

Astrid and Ris turned back toward Honor.

"Look. I'm sorry. I'm used to people being curious about Fillerra, not me. I could probably use a couple of friends," she said with a tired look in her eyes.

Astrid and Ris sat back down quietly.

"So...what are you reading?" Astrid asked.

"Time's Grudge," she replied glancing at the book. Even though they had notetablets, many still loved the feeling of turning the thick pieces of palare.

"Have you read it? Nevermind, that's a stupid question. Of course you haven't. You're from Akayta, and it was written post-war. I bought a copy of it from our book shop. It's Veleen."

Astrid smiled, "What's it about?"

"It's...an interesting book to say the least. It's about our 'long lost' time-traveling ability. Completely fiction. The book is intriguing. It follows the adventures of a girl named Rain. She's caught in the middle of the civil war that split Atoa into Akayta, Velee, and Fillerra. She discovers that we all have the ability to time-travel."

"Is it good?"

"So far...the emotional journey of the protagonist seem very realistic to me."

Astrid's heart rose into her throat. *Because you were caught in the middle of a civil war.*

"Do you want to borrow it sometime?" Honor asked.

"Sure!" Astrid replied.

"What are your favorite books?"

"Hmm...That's a hard one. I love to read. Let's see...I like *Prosper and Another Way Gone...* I know. My favorite book is *Verity*. It's about a girl who won't stop working toward her goal of saving an alternate realm from destruction. I admire her determination. You know, I think characters in books can be very inspirational," Astrid replied.

"There's no doubt about that," Honor said with a small smile.

Ris looked thoughtful. "I was just going to take Astrid to the Avocation Hall. Do you want to come?"

"I never step foot in the place."

"Are you sure?" Astrid asked.

Honor paused. "Alright. Only this time though." She got up and put her book in a brown messenger bag at her side.

Ris smiled.

They both followed Ris's blonde head through the streets of the complex for a while.

Finally a large, square building came into view. Astrid gasped. It was remarkably different from the white structures surrounding it. The light gleamed off its shiny shades of purple and blue. She could hear the noise from inside all the way out to where she was hovering.

"And that is the Avocation Hall," Ris said with satisfaction. "It's my number one, favorite place in the entire world."

"Wow. What's inside?"

"I'll show you," she said with a laugh, swimming quickly through the automatic doors. When they entered Astrid felt like she was plunged into an entirely different world. They were in a massive room structured like a hallway. Along the sides, various things were happening. A loud noise sent shivers down her back.

Music— sweeping, heartfelt music— was being played by three merpeople on a stage to the side. Her head seemed to be spinning every which way as she tried to take in all of the things that were going on.

The first thing that she saw (besides the musicians) was an area full of sculptures. Two sculptors sat with their tools, gracefully chipping the stone into different shapes.

Next, on the right side of the hallway was a marble area, where merpeople were dancing to the smooth music being poured out from the musician's fingers. The sound engulfed her.

After that was something Astrid didn't understand. It was a big machine with two metal pieces extending out of it, one to the right, one to the left.

"What is that?" she asked in amazement.

"That's my favorite part of the hall. Come on!"

With that she pulled Astrid up to the machine, then she put her hand onto a pad and closed her eyes. There were eight more pads like it. Astrid cautiously followed Ris's example and placed her hand on the pad, closing her eyes.

Suddenly she felt her mind being drawn into something. Colors flashed before her eyes and formed into a mountain. But she was floating on the mountain, looking down into a current of purple water.

"What's this?" she asked Ris in confusion.

She laughed happily. "It's The Paradise. The planet that Rune has discovered. Once we strain the last inklings of prejudice from Dalanda, we will go to The Paradise and populate it. There are so many wonderful things about it, Astrid! You're only seeing a small part of its beauty right now."

A feeling of dread settled in Astrid's stomach. She didn't know why, but something felt wrong.

"How do I get out of this?" she asked in panic, her breath becoming ragged.

Ris looked at her in confusion. "All you have to do is pull your hand away. I don't know why you would want to get out of it this early though…There's a bit of a jolt at first, but it will be gone soon."

Astrid realized that her hand was still extended, even in this simulation. She quickly pulled it back, and the view faded away, leaving her in the Avocation Hall. She felt shaken. It was just… all wrong.

Ris pulled her hand away and opened her eyes, frowning. "Why did you decide to leave?"

"I just…didn't like it," she said.

There was no reasonable explanation, but it felt deceitful to her. The powerful pull it exuded was frightening.

Ris smiled dismissively. "Like I said, it can be pretty shocking the first time."

Honor snorted. "Shocking is right. I feel the same way about it, Astrid. That's why I haven't come here since then," she said.

Astrid smiled at her understandingly. As Ris continued to show her the various attractions, Astrid kept thinking about her experience. It had certainly been beautiful, but it felt too good to be true.

She shook her head. *I'm too suspicious.*

The hall contained a cafeteria, and games of all kinds. It was fun, but by the time she was done, Astrid was more than ready to go to bed. After she said goodbye to Honor and Ris, she swam back to her assigned room in one of the residential buildings.

As soon as she turned off the lights, she got in bed. She wanted to spend time thinking about all that had happened in the past few days, but her body refused and went right to sleep.

CHAPTER EIGHT

The guider sat in his office in the Star Tribe complex, memories bombarding him with pain.

He was only nine years old. The small boy swam through his neighborhood, quickly, silently, fearfully. He just hoped he wouldn't be seen as he tugged the hood of his cloak up nervously. A hand grabbed his shoulder, and he knew that his hopes had been in vain.

"Hold on there, little eleven,*" a mocking voice said, stressing the last word.*

"You think you can just swim around our streets, littering it with your dirty presence?" the voice growled, spinning the small boy around to face him. The teenage boy glared, his smile lit with malice. His orange hair floated in a tangle of curls and the symbol of a one marked his arm like a burning reminder of what the small boy would never be.

It was Endeavour. Dev for short. One of the many people who made it their mission to make him miserable.

"Please stop, I..." the small boy began, looking down to show the proper submission, hoping that Dev would somehow decide to show mercy. But no, it just made the wicked grin on his face widen.

"You shouldn't even be allowed to live, leech. Maybe I should do Akayta a service by ensuring that you never sully our roads again."

The boy wondered if this would be the time Dev made good on his threat. Dev's grip tightened so much that he could feel his own heartbeat pounding through his arm. The young boy only tried to yank away for a moment before stopping to prepare himself for what he knew was coming. It was the risk he took whenever he went out anywhere.

Dev's fist crashed into his stomach, causing him to lose breathe and give a little cry. Dev was hitting even harder than he had last time. His fists crashed into the small boy again and again. He kept on until the boy's stomach and face were bleeding. With one last malicious grin and snarky comment, he twisted one of the boy's arms the wrong way. Tears poured out of the child's eyes as he slid down onto the ground, holding his arm. With one last curse, Dev left. Everything hurt as the small boy tried to move, but eventually he made it home. None of the single digits he passed cared to help him at all, or even give him a second glance.

CHAPTER NINE

As soon as Astrid was up and about, she went to the cafeteria for breakfast. After she got some fruity blue marja, she sat down, and soon Ris joined her.

"Why are you wearing the Star uniform today?" asked Astrid, as it wasn't her normal fashion choice.

"It's required for everyone because it's monthly training day. Many of us will be doing work for our missions and Rune says it's good for us to see a representation of our unity every now and then. But onwards from that boring stuff. So...you've been here a few days, what do you think?"

"It's wonderful," she replied, but in reality she'd been asking herself the same question.

She didn't quite feel like she fit in yet, though there was no reason to feel that way. *I just have to get used to it.* Everything seemed wonderful, but mysterious at the same time. That mysterious air made Astrid feel unstable, like everything could change in an instant and she wouldn't be prepared.

"Don't worry. I know you may not be feeling secure right now. That's exactly how I felt at first, but after a while I got used to people actually being nice to me without any ulterior motives."

"Thanks," she replied with a smile.

She understands exactly how I feel. That means I'm not strange, I'm just getting used to my surroundings.

At that moment Astrid felt a change in the water. Chills ran over her arms. It was strange, like a current of electricity warning them. She saw that everyone else had stopped their conversations and were looking around alertly.

"Oh no," Ris muttered her face going pale.

"What?" asked Astrid, getting the strong sense that she didn't understand something.

"The Feeling. It's a signal Rune is sending out. It means that we need to be alert and ready to act."

Ready to act? Astrid looked around waiting for something to happen. The room was deathly silent.

"He's never sent The Feeling out before, except in training exercises," Ris muttered clutching the table with her hands.

What's happening?

All of a sudden, Rune's voice came over the speakers across the complex, as he rushed into the cafeteria, speaking into a band on his wrist. "We are under attack by the Veleens. Battle positions. Repeat, battle positions everyone."

Battle positions? What am I supposed to do? They haven't told me anything about this yet. Panic began to rise in her. She was completely unequipped. Ris jumped up and rushed off without even waiting for her. Astrid was left floating in a flurry of merpeople rushing every which way. A hand grabbed hers, firmly and warmly wrapping around her own. She looked up into Rune's eyes.

"I know you haven't been trained for this. You need to come with me now," he said with a tone of urgency.

She nodded as he led her through the halls speedily and out into the open. At that moment a large boom rang through the complex, shaking the ground and causing white dust to fall from the dome overhead. Rune kept a firm grasp on her hand. Shouts rang out all around. *What am I going to do? I should be doing something.*

Suddenly he bent down and opened a hatch in the ground that she hadn't seen until that moment. He let go of her hand and began to go through it, then he looked up, saying, "Come on."

He was completely calm. She followed him down into the darkness, closing the hatch behind her. After several minutes, she hit the ground and lights flipped on.

They were in a circular room with large monitors everywhere. Many of them showed live footage of what Astrid supposed were cameras on the outside, and inside, of the dome.

What she saw made her gasp. Hundreds of Veleens were charging the dome, attaching explosive devices to it. Astrid could feel the rumbling noises from above. Rune sat down at one of the stations and began speaking back and forth with several people. At the same time he was typing different things onto the screens with quick swipes of his fingers. *Probably giving commands.*

She continued to turn, looking at all of the monitors, which were playing live footage. One in particular caught her eye. Astrid noticed the difference because it didn't show attacking Veleens. It showed two figures. She swam closer. After a couple of minutes she realized that it was a sixty second clip playing over and over on a loop.

It was familiar. A merman with jet-black hair swam towards the dome, carrying someone in his arms. *Mist and I,* she realized as she watched the clip. He approached and gently set her down on the sandy ground. His eyes became gentle as he gazed down at her. As he stood up, he looked straight at the camera and said something. The noise of the attack was coming from the various cameras, so she had to get closer and wait until the clip reached that part once again.

"I'm giving her to you so you can take care of her. She's been poisoned by the Veleens with densbane. I wouldn't give this responsibility to you if it were anyone else, but I know you won't harm Astrid because of the soft spot you've always had for her. I believe it's the only soft spot left in that cold heart of yours. If I'm wrong, then so be it, but if you harm her in *any* way, small or great," a protective light entered his eyes, "you will have to answer to me. You claim I am a criminal, and you know I've never once harmed you. You have done many things to me, but I still haven't done anything to you. But if she is hurt, that will change. She's mine to protect. I just hope she won't be fooled by your lies."

Astrid stood in shock, listening to what Mist had said over and over. Then she glanced back at

Rune, who was still calling out commands. She obviously wasn't supposed to see this. A wave of emotions pummeled her. She listened to the speech once more, chills running down her spine. *Rune is my friend, I can't just abandon him because his twin brother, who I've never known, implies that he is underhanded. I'm loyal. I won't abandon him. And Rune having...a soft spot for me? What did Mist mean, "She's mine to protect?"*

There were two things that kept ringing through her mind over and over and over again. The first was the expression in Mist's eyes as he laid her on the ground. The softness they gained when he looked at her. The second was the last thing he'd said. It kept coursing through her head. *"I just hope she won't be fooled by your lies."*

What lies? Is Mist lying in hopes that I would see this? Probably not. *Rune didn't tell Ris and the other nurse about this. They were surprised when I said Mist brought me here.*

It all made her wonder about everything. Mist. Rune. The Paradise. Rune's plan. Her friendships. Confusion rushed through her. She knew she wasn't seeing the whole picture, but she didn't know how to find it. Everything felt so unsure. *I am truly alone. Rune might be worthy of my trust, but I can't bring myself to give it to him right now.*

At that moment a particularly loud blast shook the underground operations center, reminding her of the present. Another one crashed right after it. The ground began to shift and shake in the equivalent of a small earthquake.

"Hold on, Astrid!" Rune shouted as a blast threw him out of his chair and onto the ground next to her.

She bent down next to him in alarm. "Are you alright?"

"I think my arm is injured," he said, rubbing it and hissing through his teeth. The blasts kept coming. She sat down next to him as dust began to float from the ceiling. Then all of the lights went out, leaving them in darkness, except for one of the monitors. She felt on edge, very on edge, but Astrid didn't feel afraid anymore.

"Come in, Spark. Come in. Come in," he said into his wristband. It only bubbled with static. "Our computer and com systems are down. We can't do anything."

No, we have to do something. This feels like giving up. "Couldn't we go up there and help?"

"No, the Veleens have certainly broken through the dome by now. We wouldn't be of any use," he said firmly.

The blasts continued, coming closer. Anger blazed in her chest. Despite what he said, she knew she should be helping. Her fear for Ris and Honor rose. She stood up. "My friends are up there. I can't just let them die. They are fighting a war and the very least we can do is be with them."

It was a fight for her to get the words out, she was so used to doing what she was told. That's what she was expected to do in Akayta, and that mindset took time to break.

He stared at her in the dim light. "We have to accept our inability to help. There's a point where we can't do anymore, and this is that point."

She sank back down, tears beginning to spill as she struggled to quash down her frustration.

His good arm lifted up and reached toward her face. He hesitated a second before brushing her cheek with his fingers. Her heart rose into her throat at his touch.

"I hope we can get out of this, Astrid, but I don't know if we will. I want you to know...I've admired you for a long time." His hand moved through her hair. "What I'm trying to say is that...I love you. I have since the first time I saw you."

Astrid nearly gasped. *He loves me?* Her feelings mixed. *Do I love him?* She wasn't sure about it. The shock took over. She was speechless. *This is not the time for this conversation.*

"You just need to know that."

His hand lowered from her face. He didn't seemed disappointed, he seemed content. So much was happening at once. Her heart yearned for that love, but she wasn't sure whether he was the one. She didn't know how long it would take to figure out when the right man came along, but she didn't want to force something that wasn't there. At that moment another boom shook the bunker. She fought the urge to swim out the hatch and help, somehow.

Guilt settled in her soul as she sat there, even if it had only been a few minutes. *No. This isn't right.* Astrid couldn't stand it anymore. She got up and, using the light from the monitor, began swimming towards the hatch.

"What are you doing?" Rune asked in confusion.

She turned back to him. "Helping my friends."

"Astrid, stop." He stood up. "You can't. You'll die," he said forcefully.

She had to make herself move. *I have to learn to act for myself, not blindly follow orders.*

"I'm going," she choked out, then swam toward the hatch.

She came to the hatch, took a deep breath, and threw it open. Instantly, laser fire flew over her head. She looked around in horror. She'd emerged into a flurry of white dust and sand. Most of the buildings were in ruins. Two fronts were fighting, the Veleens and the Star. The Veleens were shooting lasers and holding large metal shields. The case was the same with the Star, except for the fact that they didn't have the will to fight. Morale was down and they weren't receiving any orders. The situation seemed absolutely hopeless. The shield of a fallen mermaid lay near the entrance of the hatch. She pursed her lips, snatched it, and swam out of the hole. Instantly lasers were hitting the body length shield. It surprised her so much that she nearly fell back.

"There's a hatch here! Star, swim down the hole!" She yelled at the top of her voice.

She'd done a quick calculation, and all the tribe members in the immediate vicinity would fit in the room. Yes, it would be crowded and yes, it would be dark, but at least they would be safe for a little while. *It's our best chance.*

Astrid was almost on the front lines as she stood in before the hatch. *I have to guard it. If the Veleens get past this point, then it'll be hard to get back here.* Merpeople wearing the black Star shirts, giving her both confused and relieved looks, began to swim down the hole. She heard a swish behind her. Turning her head, she caught sight of Rune, who had taken up a shield.

"Everyone. Down the hatch!" he shouted.

The flow of merpeople going down the hole continued. The Veleens closed in as merpeople at the front lines began dropping their shields and plunging down into the bunker.

"I told you not to come up here!" Rune said angrily as they defended the hatch from the advancing Veleens.

"I can't let innocent people die while I cower in safety."

He looked sideways, his eyes dark. Astrid glanced around, *Only one more person to get into the bunker...* She took one last glance around to make sure there were no others nearby. Her eye caught a mermaid wearing the black shirt of the Star.

The girl was still fifty feet away from the entrance, and the Veleens were gaining on her fast. The mermaid turned her head to look at her goal. Her pale, young face and familiar blue eyes caught Astrid's attention. *Ris.* Another group of Veleens moved in to cut her off. Her back was exposed because she was holding her shield in front of her body. She would be shot down in an instant, Astrid realized. *No!* She rushed towards Ris, getting there just before they were cut off by the Veleens.

"What are you doing?" Ris asked in panic.

"Helping you. Back to back. We can get through them."

"It's impossible! They'll shoot us down!" she cried out, her voice rising in pitch with panic.

"We need to move," she replied firmly

They were back to back, Astrid facing the hatch. She pushed through the Veleen merpeople with her shield as hard as she could. Lasers pounded against them. They were only thirty feet from the entrance, fifteen, they were there. Rune was there and joined in.

"Go down, both of you!" she shouted.

Ris plunged down, then Rune. Finally, she entered the dark hole once again, locking the hatch. Pounding instantly began raining down on it. *I hope it's strong,* Astrid thought, shaking her head about the precarious nature of the situation. Rune swam up beside her and stuck something onto it.

"This will lock it more securely," he said, his voice tired, the anger completely gone.

"Are you mad at me?" she asked, turning to him.

"Not anymore. You did what was...right."

He sounds almost...grudging. Astrid thought. Then they swam down into the dark room.

CHAPTER TEN

The room was dimly lit by the computer monitors. They were all standing in the extremely crowded space. Small murmurs of conversation floated about in the water. Astrid stood by Ris. It had only been a short while since the retreat.

"Thanks for saving me. I didn't know what to do out there," Ris said, her light blonde hair hanging in tangles, covered with the sand thrown up during the attack.

"No problem." *There was no way that I was going to do nothing*, she thought.

A couple of engineers were tinkering with the computers, trying to access the cameras so that they could tell whether the Veleens were gone. The pounding had long since stopped on the sturdy hatch. It had held.

Astrid made her way over to them. "Maybe I could help?" she asked shyly.

"Give it a try," replied one of the mermen.

She bent down and looked under one of the computers. The wires were a mess. *Whoever put this computer together, pieced together the sines way too quickly. Let's see...first the reactional circuits...then the delows...then the sayor lines.* She began pulling out wires and attaching them to others. Suddenly the monitor and computer blinked on. The engineers stared at her, dumbfounded, as she sat up again and the computer began to reboot.

"You're *really* good," one said, his eyebrows raised.

Astrid began turned red. She didn't know how to reply, so she quietly made her way back to Ris, then watched as they got the cameras online and started switching through the views. Words were failing her after such a day.

After a minute, Rune turned back to the crowd and began to speak, "We are all clear. The Veleens have left, meaning we can go to the refuge complex." Murmurs quickly spread through the group, but Rune continued. "Some of you may not have heard of it. The refuge complex is an exact replica of this complex, but it's there in case of emergency. If the Veleens were to follow us, they would take that one down the same way they took this one down. We need to be very careful. I'll lead the way. It's only forty-five minutes from here by swimming, but well hidden in the Eddessian Hills." With that he began to move.

Slowly everyone began to funnel up out the hole and through their broken town. The image of her fallen comrades made Astrid's stomach sink. She tried to ignore it, tried to look away, but it was her reality—and she had to deal with it. Silent tears poured out. Such an unspeakable destruction of beauty and life. She kept an eye out for signs of life among the dead. To her relief, they ran across several other large groups of survivors. Astrid trailed at the back.

What Mist said in the clip ran through her head. *"I just hope that she won't be fooled by your lies."* What Rune said about loving her...the fact that Ris almost died...it all seemed so hard to process.

Then her thoughts drifted to another subject. *How can I get the message about the melions across to such a bloodthirsty people? The Veleens will kill me if I try to say anything. But surely there are good people who need to hear it…People like Delta.*

The swim was tiring for Astrid, who'd been through so much that day. She touched her black messenger bag. It held the disk Effie gave to her. She liked to keep it with her as a reminder of her loving sister, and because of her note. It too, seemed mysterious. *Whatever you do, don't let this fall into anyone else's hands. There is more to this than it seems.*

What could that small disk contain that was so important?

The water flowed against her hands. It was water that had surrounded her for an entire lifetime. It was familiar. It had mocked her, given relief, and witnessed all of her struggles firsthand. It was always shifting, changing. She looked ahead, all of the Star were tired. They'd just been brutally attacked by the Veleens and lost the battle. *It is their suffering I should be thinking about, not mine.* Nonetheless, the sights of the battle seared their pain into her mind and made it her own.

Finally, a white dome identical to that of the complex came into view among the purple hills. After Rune unlocked the door, the exhausted string of merpeople filtered in. The only difference that Astrid could see was that this dome smelled and felt completely new. It had never been lived in.

A voice beside Astrid spoke, bringing her out of her thoughts. "You saved us all."

It was a disheveled and dirt-covered Honor. Her long, dark hair hung in clumps, and the frown on her long face was deeper than usual.

"No...just..."

"You don't have to pretend it didn't happen. You were brave enough to save us."

Astrid couldn't bring herself to smile at the compliment. There was a fact she'd been avoiding. Rune was going to let them all die. If she hadn't stepped in, they would've been killed. *The Rune I knew would never do anything like that.* She tried to stop that line of thought. *Maybe I misunderstood him.* In her heart she knew she hadn't. Astrid glanced at Honor. Her face and bearing said it all. *She's not meant to be a soldier.* Her shoulders were slumped and she looked so disheartened that Astrid wanted to cry. She understood the need for each person in such a small community to be a soldier...but still.

She put a hand on Honor's shoulder. "It's going to be okay."

Honor turned to her, desperation filling her eyes, "How can you say that? The Veleens will just keep attacking! We *want* to believe we're making progress, but I don't see it. I feel like we're going around in circles."

Astrid shook her head. "We have to hope, Honor. Without hope we *will* fail."

"I don't know. This doesn't feel right." She lowered her voice. "I feel like Rune needs to tell us all his supposedly glorious plan. Every last detail of it. Or even just a general outline would be fine. I don't like feeling like I'm blind and I hate being in the dark. Besides, what would happen if he died? All of our work would go to waste."

Astrid agreed with her. "Then you need to talk to him about it."

Honor gave one of her snort laughs. "He may be accessible to you, Astrid, but most of us can't talk with him unless he summons us."

This shocked Astrid. *In a situation such as this, a leader should be accessible to his own people.*

"I'll talk to him then."

"Talking isn't going to change anything. He's going to continue doing everything the way he's been doing it. The way he's *always* done it."

Astrid shook her head. "I'm not sure about anything right now. He hasn't always been this way, Honor."

She went to her assigned apartment and, after freshening up, headed down to the cafeteria. At the unspoken requests of the cafeteria workers, everyone pitched in to begin breaking out the backup supplies. Soon they were done, and the room was packed with people eating. Astrid swam to a corner and sat down on the ground since there were no open chairs. She barely touched her food as she watched everyone swim around and talk, oblivious to her presence. She finally placed her uneaten food on the ground beside her and hugged her fin to herself, sighing.

She brought the silver disk out of her bag and examined it once again. *So beautiful, but not anything to guard with your life.*

A voice suddenly spoke, startling her, and causing her to drop the disk.

"I'm sorry," Rune said as he bent down and then handed it back to her with a curious glance.

"Oh. It's alright." She turned red as she got up.

"I need to talk to you about something," he said, looking her straight in the eye.

For some reason a feeling of dread began to fill her stomach. "Yes?"

"I've given you an assignment."

CHAPTER ELEVEN

Rune continued, "We're going to begin training you tomorrow." With that he abruptly turned to go.

Astrid stared in amazement. *But...it's so soon.* She swallowed and called after Rune, who was moving away. "Wait…"

He turned back.

"What's the assignment?"

"You won't know until after you've been trained. That way we can get a better idea of your strengths and weaknesses. The mind is very powerful, Astrid. If you know what your goal is, you won't strive to be better than that goal requires."

"But…"

"Astrid. I know what you're capable of. You have no excuses. Meet me tomorrow morning at six sharp, right outside the central building." His voice was hard as he turned and swam away, leaving her gaping in astonishment.

I don't know why he thinks I'll be good at whatever job he's giving me. I'd better go get some rest. Why is he so aggravated? She slowly got up, and after disposing of her food, headed back to her apartment to sleep. *One thing is for sure. I'll do my best.*

As she was about to enter her room, the door to the next room opened and Honor emerged.

She looked up in surprise. "Astrid. I was actually just coming to find you."

Astrid went ahead and opened the door to her apartment, then ushered Honor inside. They both sat down in silence. Honor stared out into the distance, her black hair moving in front of her face. *Her mind is occupied.* After several minutes Honor glanced up, startled, and remembered where she was.

She blushed slightly, "Sorry."

"It's alright. I can tell you're tired."

Honor gave her a little smile of understanding. She held a beautifully bound book out to Astrid, who carefully took it. "I wanted to lend *Time's Grudge* to you."

"Thank you. So you finished it?"

"Yes."

"What did you think?"

She smiled, "I don't want to spoil it for you, but it was wonderful. It tore me apart and then mended me back together. I'm not sure if you're familiar with the history of Atoa, but it's interesting how accurate the details are. It makes it feel so real. It's beautifully simple, but profound."

"In other words, it just became your favorite book."

"Exactly." Honor actually grinned. That was the first time Astrid had seen her sadness fall away. She sobered, "I guess I also related to the main character because of the setting of civil war."

Astrid remained quiet. She could tell from Honor's expression that she was about to share her personal experience. Honor obviously didn't do that with many people, if any at all.

She sighed, then started to speak. "Fillerra. It was a glorious tribe, full of life. Vibrant. We were great lovers of history, music, and the future. Time was our main area of study. We had libraries filled with millions of books. The older generation was fading into the background and letting the younger ones lead. As it should be. We were happy...until." She sighed. "There always seems to be an "until," doesn't there?"

She pulled her tail up under her on the big fluffy chair, then continued. "Unrest had apparently been boiling under the surface for some time. A growing faction of people were unhappy. They insisted we'd departed from the goals and form of government our ancestors had broken away from Atoa to gain. They called themselves the Truists. More and more people joined their cause." Bitterness filled her voice. "We were happy. Everyone was prospering and our government was operating fine for us. Then, like I said, the Truists persuaded many people to side with them. We lost sight of the fact that, though we may not have been following our ancestors' vision for the perfect government, our government was working fine for us.

"The leaders on both sides rose up and argued. Eventually the protests turned violent. The Truists put together a military. That was it. Things only went downhill from there. Fighting began in the city. The blood of innocent people flooded the streets. It ripped families apart like they were made of palare. Some members would side with the Truists, others with the government. When faced with that decision in battle, they ended up literally fighting and killing each other. Hate filled everything, everything, Astrid. Infrastructure was destroyed and the city fell apart. It went on for three years, and by that point we were in ruins.

"Then came the day when the Fillerran tribe finally fell. I call it The Final Extinguishment. I apparently get to name it since I'm the only one left to write the history books," she said bitterly. "Anyway, it was a day of many battles. Then there was the fire."

Astrid gasped, "Fire?" She'd only read about it in books. The subject had always fascinated her. She'd read several scientific theories about the possibility of sustained fire. An area so high in temperature a visual phenomenon appeared. A blaze could start if there was a big enough explosion to generate a flame, and if it was continually fed magnesium to keep it burning. But she'd never heard of a fire raging through a city.

"It was horrible. It was bright white and spread through the city quickly, devastating everything in its path. Of course the people had no idea how to stop it— and before they even thought of that, they had to figure out what it was. We'd never experienced anything like it. I'm still not sure how it started, but I think some explosives must've malfunctioned. I heard several large bangs right before I saw the fire. It began burning the magnesium in the indigo sand of the tribe—the very thing that made Fillerra unique, killed it. I was just outside the city, writing at the time, so I swam for my life. A ring of talena rock surrounds Fillerra, which kept the fire, the destruction, from spreading any farther.

When I got further away, I turned and watched my home ablaze in white flames. Screams rang out into the sky. And that was the day Fillera died."

Tears flowed from her eyes, even though she grimaced trying to stop them. One of her hands went up to her face and she began to sob brokenly.

The horror of what Honor had experienced settled over Astrid. She reached over and touched her shoulder. "Fillerra isn't dead, its culture and story live in you."

Honor shook her head violently, "I try to forget it, but I can't. My entire family died. My way of life died. I try to forget the horrors of those last few years, but they seem to occupy my thoughts night and day. I want to remember my family, Astrid! I want to remember my friends and the good times, but it's all overshadowed by the war and fire. And through it all, I'm constantly afraid that somehow I will forget, and Fillerra will be totally forgotten."

"That's horrible. I'm sorry. I'm not going to pretend to understand how much you struggle, but you can know that I'll be here for you. If you ever need to talk about it more, I'm here."

"You are a true friend," said Honor.

Astrid just smiled sadly. "Maybe if you wrote your experiences down, the good and bad, it would help you feel better. You wouldn't feel like you were in danger of forgetting."

Honor's face brightened, "That's a good idea. I think I'll do that." She sighed and got up, "I'll let you get some sleep now."

Astrid smiled and rose, then showed her to the door. "Goodbye, Honor."

"Bye, Astrid. And thank you."

As Astrid brushed her hair out and got ready for bed, she felt lucky. She had been oppressed, yes. She had been hurt emotionally, yes. She had lost family, yes. But she hadn't had to watch an entire society be destroyed. She hadn't had to see total, complete bloodshed and decimation.

After brushing the salt buildup off of her tail, she got into bed and turned off the light. She lay there for several hours, her mind refusing to slow down. The day had been exhausting. So much had happened. The fact that Rune had been ready to let the Star die still bothered her. *How could he do that? He was cowering in the safety of his bunker while his people died.* She quickly fell to sleep and entered a dream.

CHAPTER TWELVE

They sat on a strip of sparkling, crystalline blue sand.

Astrid put down the history book she'd been reading out loud. "What do you think Sign's feelings were when he was a double agent?"

Rune crossed his arms. "I think he was scared. I think he was trying to learn which side he should really be on. In that position, he essentially had the power to bring down one side or the other. I doubt that he planned on ending up in a position of such power. It just happened as he was trying to find his way."

"This book paints it as though he was a terrible traitor to Akayta— but I think it's interesting that he didn't use that power to bring down either side. Instead he used the information he learned to lead another group of people away to form Fillerra," replied Astrid thoughtfully.

"He probably wasn't as bad as this paints him to be. He did what he thought was right and tried to avoid bloodshed."

"*What would you do if you were in his position?*" she asked.

"*That's hard. If I saw that neither side had a moral viewpoint, I think I would've started a new group also.*"

"*I'm sure he had many struggles because of the factions his friends and families aligned themselves with.*"

"*Everyone in the Atoan Civil War did.*"

"*How would you even begin to get out of something like that? If you believe in something and are fighting for one side, but someone very close to you firmly believes in and is fighting for the other side, then you are in essence working towards the goal of killing them.*"

"*That's why I'm glad I'm not in the middle of a civil war,*" he replied with sincerity and a touch of relief.

"*True. But the people who are faced with it have to make a decision.*"

They were both quiet for a second. Astrid stared down at the shifting blue sand. A slight, refreshing wave of cold water wafted over her.

"*What do you think Fillerra and Velee are like?*" asked Rune, looking longingly across the uninterrupted sandy plain.

"*I can't even begin to imagine. Hmm. To start with, maybe they don't mark you based upon your birth.*"

"*Maybe they have tall, colorful buildings.*"

"*Maybe they have music houses that are open to everyone.*"

Astrid smiled as she imagined all of the things that her version of a perfect society would have.

A low, echoey sound plunged through the atmosphere, interrupting her train of thought. A coldness pervaded the water and crept over Astrid. She could see from Rune's face that he felt it too. They turned around.

The sight before them took her breath away. Great billows of dirty water swirled through the atmosphere. It filled the entire visible plain behind them, obscuring Akayta from view. The cloud was on them before they had time to react. It whisked over them with force. Dirt spewed into her eyes as the storm began to move her.

"Rune! We need to stay together! Where are you?" she shouted with all of her might, despite the sand flying into her mouth. She looked for any sign of him, shielding her eyes and holding out her hand. Within the storm, all things were blurred from sight. She couldn't see very far in front of her.

Then, through the blur, his hand reached out and caught hers. They pulled together, and huddled, keeping their eyes closed. The storm was harsh, but as Astrid held Rune's hand, she had the assurance that she was not alone. Just the fact that he was present brought her comfort.

Finally the storm passed, leaving dust and dirt floating in tiny circles throughout the water. Astrid took a deep breath and opened her eyes. She laughed as she took her hand out of Rune's and studied him. He was covered in sand and dirt, which struck her as utterly comedic.

He grinned. "We are a sight."

She looked down at herself and laughed harder, realizing she was in the same state. He glanced toward Akayta. Though the storm had passed them by, it still obscured the city-state. They would have to wait for it to pass there, too, before heading home.

In those minutes while the storm was passing, Astrid felt exhilaration and fear, but she also felt support in the knowledge that she and Rune had gone through it together. There was no doubt either of them would do anything and everything to help the other. And that would always be the case.

Astrid pulled her hair back into her usual side ponytail as she swam towards the central building. Sleep hadn't helped to calm her nerves. The feelings of the dream still ran through her. Most dreams were exact memories. A rare condition that she had made it unusual to have the normal topsy-turvy dreams everyone else experienced. They did happen occasionally, but only when she was extremely disturbed. Most were merely memories. Effie had figured that out for her. *Effie. Oh, Effie.* Soon Rune came into view.

"Come on," he said immediately.

He led her for about fifteen minutes, until they finally arrived at an open space. It looked completely empty. *What's my assignment? What will I be trained in here?* Rune bent down and roughly brushed some sand away from a particular spot on the ground. Astrid saw that he was digging up a metal box. Yanking it up, he opened it, revealing all kinds of weapons and objects.

He finally faced her, his eyes growing softer and his stern expression lifting slightly.

"You're going to learn how to fight. You'll be going on missions, and you need to be able to defend yourself and inflict harm if it's necessary...which it very well might be. Now, take this."

He tossed her an oddly shaped piece of metal. It looked like it had been torn off a random machine. Astrid barely caught it.

Her stomach turned, she didn't like the sound of this. "Rune, I don't mind learning how to defend myself, but...I don't want to hurt anyone. Not on purpose.

He calmly ignored her. "I'll teach you, but first I must see what you already know. Let's begin."

"Alright," she replied hesitantly.

He plunged toward her with a glinting knife.

"Aaa!" she screeched, holding up the strange piece of metal as a barrier in panic. Her heart raced at the shock of being attacked. A metal-on-metal sound painfully filled her ears, and Rune was knocking the metal piece out of her hands before she knew it, bending her wrists the wrong way in the process. "Ow!" she gritted out as the dust settled around her on the ground. Rune stood over her.

"You have to be quicker. Much quicker."

She got up, her heart rising into her throat in confusion. "What job would require me to fight, Rune? To really fight. To kill."

"Like I said, you'll be going on missions. You must learn to fight. You may be kind to the world, but the world won't be kind to you. You're too soft. You need to learn that not everyone will love and help you. An instinct for self-preservation has to rule you when you are faced with the choice of your own survival or that of someone else. That's the way the world works. You need to shield your emotions. Everybody can tell exactly what's going on in your head and that would be dangerous if you were captured. It's dangerous, period," he spouted.

Astrid backed up. Tears spilled out of her eyes as she tried to hold her sobs back. "You're not just talking about fighting. You think I don't know that? You really think you have the right to tell me something like that? And what happened to the person you used to be? The Rune I knew would never accept the view that a person's heart must be cold in order to avoid being hurt. That's what you're really saying."

A spark of anger flashed in his eyes once again. "No matter how much you would like to believe in a world with a good heart, it doesn't exist. This is for your benefit, you have to learn to hurt them, or the people of this world will crush you under their weight and grind you into dust," he replied with a stinging bitterness.

"I've already been crushed by society. Despite what you may think, I know what I believe. You think I'm too nice? Too soft?" Pain filled her eyes. "I know what it's like to be looked down upon, but I don't let that make me hard. I believe there are good, true people in this world like Honor, Delta, and Ris. Like my friends. I used to think you were one of them. TI must have been wrong about that." She turned and stormed away. *Honor was right. Talking is not going to make Rune change his ways. Maybe he is different. I'm not sure I like it.*

No, I know I don't.

CHAPTER THIRTEEN

Anger and tears mixed together in a formula for despair. Her feelings felt so jumbled. She was beginning to think she couldn't trust Rune. Her soul felt like it was being torn apart by confusion as she sank down against a building and let her sobs take her. *Will I ever be able to sort things out? And what about the core? Has Rune even thought about it since that day?*

But Rune was her friend. Two years ago she would have trusted him with her life, so why was she having trouble with this now?

Astrid took a deep breath. *I have to trust him. I can only do so much by myself and he can help orchestrate how I help by sending me on this mission. I have to go back and train. Maybe I don't think I can fight, but he certainly does. Besides, I do have to know how to defend myself. I said I was going to try, and so I will.*

She got up, taking a deep breath of fresh water. Astrid slowly made her way back to the training ground, wondering if he would still be there, and indeed he was. He was facing away from her, his fists clenched so hard that they were white, his back tense.

"If you are not willing to complete your training, you are not welcome here. Every member must offer some benefit to the tribe."

She choked down her tears and managed to say, "I'm ready to train."

He turned, his eyes sad. "Alright, then. We'll forget what just happened. Now, let's try again."

He plunged toward her with a knife in hand. She lunged out of the way. They sparred for hours. Finally, Rune dismissed her.

Astrid couldn't remember the last time she'd had so much exercise. Her bones were already starting to ache. She desperately needed something to distract her from her fatigue...and from Rune. Slowly she made her way to the Avocation Hall.

It surprised her to see that it was an exact duplicate of the other Avocation Hall. It even had the machine.

There were only a few people there. The musicians played a slow song which she would normally enjoy, but her mind was restless. She felt herself drawn towards the machine. Part of her wanted to plunge back into that imaginary world, but another part implored her to avoid it. She sat down on a nearby chair and watched the glistening beast of a machine and the people using it.

Faces lit up with silly grins as they immersed themselves in the fake world the machine created. Astrid watched with growing interest and a small inkling of horror. The machine changed the most solemn expressions into ridiculous grins. Astrid had no problem with people smiling, but this incredible joy on their faces wasn't natural. The simulation was beautiful, but not that beautiful or...astonishing.

Astrid's heart quickened as she, again, felt a powerful urge to immerse herself in the simulation. She bolted up from her chair as the urge became so strong that her face began to heat up and gritty salt fell from it.

She took one more glance at the machine and then swam out of the Avocation Hall as quickly as she could. Finally the feeling started to dull. She stopped swimming and found herself in front of her housing hall. Terror filled her mind and heart. When had the machine gained so much power over her? Astrid found herself still trying to steady her breathing from the frightening experience.

It was dinner time and mermaids were making their way to the cafeteria. Astrid grasped her head in her hands. She didn't feel like eating. The only thing that might relieve her tense emotional state was sleep. So she entered the building and made her way through the vacant halls. Everyone was at dinner, and most of the doors were closed. This hall was a stark white, free of the decorations that had colored the original Star Tribe quarters.

Astrid was almost to her room when she heard a voice coming from a partially opened door.

Rune. He wasn't going to dinner either. As she neared his quarters, curiosity drew her to the open door. *Who is he talking to?*

She paused and peaked through the opening. Rune stood, staring in the mirror, his hands clutching the edges of the desk beneath it.

"I'm right," he muttered to himself so desperately, so vehemently, that she knew he was trying to convince himself. His eyes burned with a fire of hatred and fear. The knuckles on his hands were white from grasping the desk so tightly.

"I will build an empire. A grand place that exceeds their petty mindsets. I'll become a legend."

He clenched his teeth.

"I will show them what an eleven can truly do. They will still hate me, but this time it will be from fear instead of mockery," he growled at himself. "This time, I'll live in comfort while they toil, building my empire. I'll pay them back with two blows for every single blow they've ever given me. I'm right. I am right."

He closed his eyes and lowered his head, pounding his hand against the desk.

Astrid shook her head in disbelief and swiftly swam past the doorway while his eyes were closed. She fought back the tears as she entered her room. Astrid was tired of crying, tired of being shocked. *Rune...Who is he now?* She feared the answer with steadily growing dread. She barred the tears from her eyes, she barred the emotions from her heart until all that remained was a faint undercurrent of disturbance. Sleep overcame her quickly, and she gladly gave in.

She felt the anger and hatred swirling through her mind. Her view was red-and-black. Fire could be good or bad. This was only bad. A fire of rage against the people who had been so cruel to her. It boiled and writhed...screaming for release. They would pay. She would show them what a sixteen could really do— the harm a sixteen could inflict. She would hurt them in every way she knew how. Verbally, physically— in all the ways they had hurt her.

"No matter how much you would like to believe in a world with a good heart, it doesn't exist! This is for your benefit, you have to learn to hurt them, or the people of this world will crush you under their weight and grind you into dust."

Repeating Rune's words, she shouted to the world as loud and far as her voice would go. All emotions were eclipsed by anger and hatred built from the hurt and the fear she'd endured.

Astrid woke with a start. She began to choke out tears. The nightmare screamed in her head as though it were still happening. She didn't want to be consumed by hate and malice. But she had the potential to end up that way. She snuggled farther under the covers and cried her heart out. She didn't want to become that. She didn't. She refused.

CHAPTER FOURTEEN

The guider pressed his hand against his head, which was pounding with pain. He sat on the bed in his room. Unease and weariness swirled through his heart as he thought about how his plan to take over Akayta and Velee was progressing.

The king of Akayta and the high commander of Velee were already under his control. Well, mostly. They'd given in due to the threat of a deadly weapon made by Cog, a notorious weapons inventor.

Just for good measure, he'd threatened them with assassination as well. For months now they had been giving him smaller hand weapons, providing food, and gathering intelligence for him.

His hold on them was loosening. The Veleens' attack, no doubt initiated by their high commander, was evidence of that.

Once he amassed a bigger group of people in the Star, he planned to take full control by force and declare himself king. He knew very well that if he tried to do that now, the leaders of Akayta and Velee would surely assassinate him. He'd started the Star so that he would have a group of people who were loyal to him. By surrounding himself with faithful followers, his chances of survival had increased.

The guider sighed and crossed his arms. A flare of anger sparked through his mind. Astrid was making this difficult. Far too difficult. If she knew...

No. He didn't want to think about that. The look in her eyes when she rushed into the din of battle, after he told her not to. The look in her eyes when he tried to explain how she should defend herself against the world. She...she didn't understand.

A tear floated out of his eye. For a moment his hatred was gone and he was just an oppressed, abused boy, crushed by the Akaytans.

He steeled himself. They would be the slaves when he was king. They would be the oppressed.

CHAPTER FIFTEEN

Astrid trained for three weeks. Rune taught her many things, from evading attacks to defending herself with whatever was at hand. He taught her to be quick, silent, and deadly if need be. Every day she felt herself getting stronger. Astrid wasn't a master, but she was efficient.

An uneasy feeling grew in the back of her mind as Rune shoved her through training exercises where she had to "kill" a dummy. She learned to kill with poison, a knife, a laser gun. *It isn't just defense.* She pushed her doubts away with all her might and replaced them with learning the skills, with being the best she could possibly be. After all, Rune was her friend. When she overheard him talking...the anger in his voice...

But she *had* to remain confident that he would never use that anger for sinister purposes.

Because if he did, she would lose everything. It would be worse than if he'd actually died. She had to trust him. But in the depths of her soul, she knew she was just lying to herself.

Her heart beat impossibly fast as she flipped backwards to avoid Rune's sword. It was much more efficient than trying to swim backwards. Panting, she deftly swung around behind him and knocked the knife out of his hand, managing to get his arms into a position where he couldn't move.

"Got you," Astrid said. She was becoming more confident in her abilities.

He turned and gave a small smile once she let him go. "You're ready. Go take a break and pack. Come back in an hour and a half and we'll send you off."

She nodded with a sigh and swam away. *Already? This is all happening so quickly.*

After she packed, she went to the cafeteria to look for Ris and Honor since it was lunchtime. They were at a table and both looked up as she sat down.

"You must have been given an assignment. I haven't seen you around lately," Ris said.

"Yeah. I'm actually leaving today."

"Well, good luck!" Ris replied brightly.

"More like don't kill anyone," Honor muttered, looking down into her noasé.

Astrid looked toward her in confusion. "What?"

Honor shook her head, making her black hair move slightly. "Nevermind."

What Honor said bothered her. *What could she mean?* She quickly picked the conversation back up. "Have you ever been on a mission, Honor?"

"No. I've been here for two years, but haven't received one yet. And I hope I never will," she said darkly, then quickly continued in an overly bright way, "I'm perfectly happy with my job as records keeper, and I may be a coward, but I don't want to leave it."

Astrid studied her. The second part didn't sound like something Honor would say at all. *What does she mean by she hopes she won't get an assignment?* She shook herself out of her thoughts and got up.

"Well, I have to go."

"Good luck until then!" Ris turned back to her food.

Honor stared into her eyes seriously, not smiling the least bit. "You have the choice," she mouthed before turning back to her food speedily, with a demeanor that almost spoke of fear.

Astrid just gaped at her for a moment before she forced herself to move on. *You have the choice.* It rang through her head over and over. Honor obviously knew something she didn't.

Finally she reached the training ground once more. Rune was waiting for her. There was a moment of silence as they evaluated each other.

"I knew you could do it, but you learned faster and better than I expected," he said with a genuine smile.

Astrid grinned back. She felt like she had her friend back. At least for a moment. Things were going to be fine. Rune may have gone astray in some ways, but he was still her friend.

"Are you ready for your mission?"

"Very," she replied, taking a deep breath.

"Alright then. You're going to be on call in Velee. One of our people there says she asked around and you've been largely forgotten. So you should be safe. Occasionally there are people that pose a threat to our plan. Your job will be to eliminate them," he said casually.

At that moment Astrid's world changed for good. It felt like her life had shattered, and pieces of it were cutting her as they rained down on her head. She was careful to keep her face neutral, but her emotions raged like a storm. *Assassin? He*

135

wants me to be an assassin. No. No. I must not have heard right. Except...she did. *Rune isn't the same. He's become cold, just like Mist said.*

She felt betrayed, and that betrayal sank deep into her heart. His face flashed into her mind as she remembered all the times they'd taken comfort in each other over the years. All the times she'd looked into his eyes and felt that everything would be alright. He had helped her maintain the belief that not everyone in the world was cruel, that not everyone in the world wanted to hurt her.

Her heart was breaking in two. Rune had changed. He had become the opposite of everything he'd been before. He was now cruel and self-centered. Hard. Cold. She felt tears rise in her throat that she desperately wanted to let out. Rune. The loss was too great to have to endure again in a way even worse than before.

She quickly sorted through her options and forced herself to realize that she might be in danger if she refused the mission. Who knew what this new Rune with a dangerous glint in his eyes would do? *I can't get out of the complex. The dome is caging me in, so I just have to play along for now and wait for a chance...a chance to run.*

She was careful to keep her face neutral as he studied her, then continued, "I'll contact you on this device when you need to eliminate a target." He handed her a rectangular tablet.

She swallowed, trying to keep her hands from trembling as she took it.

"Until then, you will find a place to stay and a way to support yourself, but to start you off I'll give you fifty Veleen onants. That should be enough to buy housing and food for two or three months. The very first thing you'll need to do though is dye your hair and change your appearance. Just to ensure no one will recognize you." He handed her a small bag that clanked when she took it.

All of her tears wanted to flow out. Her sobs tried to explode, but she knew she couldn't let them.

She had to take a moment before saying, "Alright."

I've been trained as an assassin. She tucked the tablet and money into the bag she'd packed with her few belongings.

"Come on. I have to open the gate for you," he said, swimming off.

Astrid followed, forcing herself to keep her breathing even. When they reached the gate, Rune used a card to open it. Outside was the same blue and sandy world she knew, but it looked so wide. So big.

"I programmed the coordinates of Velee into your tablet," he said.

"Thank you," she managed to get out.

His green eyes seemed to drill into hers as he smiled slightly. "Once we've successfully taken over and corrected the oppressive attitudes of the Veleens and Akaytans, we'll move to a beautiful planet I have chosen. We won't have to deal with these people anymore. But we have to take it one step at a time. You will be a big part of this movement. You'll be remembered as a hero, Astrid."

A hero and an assassin are very different things. She answered with a false smile.

He touched her hair briefly then turned and went back inside the dome, the door closing behind him.

I can't run away yet, there are cameras everywhere. I've got to look like I'm going to Velee. It's my best option. What will I do? This all seems so hopeless. I just have to take it one step at a time. She pulled out the tablet. As soon as the power was on, the coordinates popped up and it began to guide her. She swam as fast as she could. The lump in her throat made it hard to breathe.

After swimming for two hours she reached the outskirts of Velee. She continued to swim onward, having no idea where she was going. *No destination. Just like my life. Nowhere to hide. Why do I still want to save these people? It's obviously up to me and Effie to tell everyone about the core.*

The core. Nobody's listening. We're all going to die anyway. She could barely hold the pain inside her throbbing, breaking heart. She swam and swam and swam, her heart boiling with anger and fear and hurt.

Being lost in the noisy Veleen crowd made her feel sick. A familiar voice caught her ears and she turned to look at the platform in the city center. The high commander in all of his arrogant pomp. She stopped, letting people push past her as she listened to him drone on about the recent events in their "ancient and orderly democracy." Her eyes wandered over the faces in the crowd.

One face in particular caught her eye. A girl. She looked familiar. *Where have I seen her?* It bothered Astrid. Something bothered her about that face being out of place. *I know. She's a part of the Star.*

At that moment Astrid saw the arm rise. She saw the gun in the hand of the Star. She lunged forward in horror as the sound resounded. She watched the laser fly through the water and straight into the high commander's body.

"No!" she shouted in horror as he fell to the bottom of the platform, dead.

Dead. *Killed.* Killed by the Star. Simultaneous shouts rang out every which way. People moved in a manic frenzy as the culprit set off some sort of contamination bomb that Astrid began to choke on. *They killed him. They just...killed him.* Astrid didn't like him as a person, but she didn't want him to die.

The water all around her was clouded. The hectic motions of the crowd made her turn in so many directions, trying to figure out what to do, while still processing the trauma. Tears floated out of her eyes. So many faces...so many faces rushing past. A blur of conflicting noises and colors. Confusion blurred her mind as she choked.

Then she spotted another familiar face. Green eyes lighting up in surprise as he saw her. A mask slipped over her mouth and nose to filter out the fog. A hand on her shoulder urging her to move. As they struggled through the smoke, a strong sense of relief hit her.

Together. Struggling through it together.

Tears continued to pour out. *How can I change any of this? How can I make a difference when no one will listen and I can't trust anyone?* She tried to calm her sobs as she closed her eyes in agony. *I'm trying to help everyone, but I'm just one person. How much of a difference can I actually make?* Her life, her goals...everything seemed to be broken, lying on the ground in scattered pieces. *Where can I even start?*

She continued to scramble through the fog with him. It surrounded her and swirled, the commotion around them deafening. The noise began to fade. The fog disappeared and they both collapsed in an alley. As they took off their masks, they turned to face each other.

CHAPTER SIXTEEN

"What are you doing back here?"

She wasn't shocked when she saw that it was Mist, though she should've been. A minute of silence prevailed as they stared at each other, both of them hot and panting from escaping the contamination bomb. Jolting emotions rose in her as she remembered waiting out the dust storm with Rune years ago, and wading through the fog with Mist just a second ago.

"What are you doing back here?" he repeated.

Astrid took deep breaths as mixed feelings swept through her. *Rune said Mist was a criminal. Then again, he did help me...and Rune may have been lying.*

No, he probably was *lying.*

Mist's earnestness in the video flashed back into her mind. *Well, I'm more inclined to trust Mist. I'd better be careful though—I was wrong about Rune.* She sighed, tears welling up in her throat. *I was wrong about Rune.*

"Why did you help me again?" she asked cautiously.

He crossed his arms and leaned against the wall. "I was watching the high commander's speech and then I saw you. I should have known that Rune would try to use your drive for excellence to his advantage."

"My drive for excellence? How would you know anything about me?" Her face displayed her growing anxiety. Astrid felt like she'd been hit by a transport.

He smiled genuinely. "That's what makes you such a great scientist. I always saw it in you."

"How...I never even knew Rune *had* a twin brother. I certainly didn't meet you."

His green eyes softened as he gazed at her and swam a bit closer. Her heart jumped and tears threatened once more.

In that moment she knew. His face right before her, yearning for acceptance.

"Your name isn't Mist. It's Rune," she whispered.

He nodded as he smiled softly. "It's me."

She hugged him and started sobbing as everything that she had experienced that day overwhelmed her.

"That wasn't you. The Rune in the complex...he didn't seem like you at all, but I thought he was. I thought...you had changed."

His arms closed around her, making her feel safe in their hold.

He pulled away and put his hand on her face. Rune's touch felt right, unlike his twin's.

"Astrid."

They both felt the joy of finally being in the other's presence once again. And they both knew exactly what the other was trying to say. *It's been so long. I missed you terribly.*

"I had a feeling I'd see you again." His smile was soft.

"Why did you tell me your name was Mist, and why did you take me to the complex?" she whispered.

"Mainly because I didn't have the medical supplies to save you, and I knew Cipher did. I knew that if I told you my true identity, you'd want to come with me. It wasn't safe for you in Velee, and I knew you had a better chance of surviving if I took you to the Star. So that's what I did. Mist is the codename I use in Velee."

A moment of silence settled.

"I'm so glad to see you. Everything was so lonely after you left," said Astrid.

"For me too," he said.

Astrid felt herself calming down. Now she wasn't alone. This was her Rune, and he wasn't going to leave her for dead or betray her. Ever. And she felt the same way. As she gazed at his face and messy black hair, she realized just how much she'd missed him. The real him. *This is him. I can feel it.* The relief she felt at this revelation knew no bounds.

Then Astrid remembered her questions.

"Why would it be dangerous to be associated with you and why is your brother using your name?"

"Come on." He took her hand. "I'll explain on the way."

She nodded, taking his warm hand and starting to follow. "Wait a second," she said, stopping. She dug into her bag and pulled out the tablet. "Your brother gave this to me. I'm sure it can be tracked, and I definitely don't want him tracking me." She tossed the tablet into the alley, then placed her hand in his once again.

"Alright, let's go,"

As soon as they began to move, Rune spoke. "Cipher, my brother, was in hiding in Akayta for four years. He started stealing expensive jewelry right before I met you and was on the run from the police officials. We were very close. He managed to see me every day. He was a master at avoiding the cameras, and sometimes I helped short out the ones in our house for an hour, so he could come in.

"He changed though. Cipher was tired of being oppressed as a red-and-black and he wanted to do something to the people who were despising us. That was his motive for thievery. I could see he wasn't satisfied with the extent of his crimes.

"Then Nora was killed and he went over the edge. That's what started to pull us apart. We argued over it all the time.

"Sometimes, when you would come to visit, he was there. He would hide in a closet and listen to us. Over time he came less and less often, because of our differing views. But he told me the reason he stayed at all was because of you. You intrigued him to no end. One day, about a year later, he decided to leave for Velee."

Astrid grimaced. That was an uncomfortable thought...and a creepy one. Her thoughts moved on.

After a moment she asked, "Why did you leave without me?"

Rune's eyes grew sad and angry. "On the day I left, Astrid, I had no choice. The police officials took me in and showed recordings of me saying things that "could spark rebellion"...like when I told you not to let the mark hold you back. I had three infractions, and because of that, they regarded me as a threat. I wasn't careful because I didn't think the things I said were a big deal. But it makes sense when I think about it. They're completely intolerant of double digits trying to stand up for themselves."

Astrid nodded. The Akaytans put cameras in most public places. It was also required that an occupied house have one in every room. If a person was determined, they could manage to skirt the areas that were monitored.

When Effie moved to her apartment, Astrid remained in their parents' house. Because it had been built over one hundred years ago, the house had no market value for Akaytans, who mainly liked new, shiny things. So it was fairly normal for Effie to retain ownership, and not try to sell it. Effie had filled out the paperwork to send Astrid off to the the double digit sector. Therefore, that's where the government thought she was. Luckily, they didn't monitor the number of people in the double digit sector. They weren't worth the effort.

Since there was supposedly no one living in the house, the government didn't bother wasting resources to keep the cameras on. Thus, Astrid was free to carry out her experiments. She always exited the back way, and took an unmonitored route, so her secret residence wouldn't be discovered.

Punishments were severe for the smallest infractions in Akayta...especially when it came to people of the lower classes.

Astrid's attention was drawn back to Rune as he continued his story.

"Anyway, on the way to the prison to be executed, I managed to break free of the guards. They chased me, but I was able to stay ahead of them. They only stopped after I was well beyond the limits of the city. I wanted to get you, or at least say goodbye, but I knew it was too risky. If I did, you might've also been convicted because of their prejudice. It wasn't like Cipher's thieving shenanigans where he would just be beaten to within an inch of his life. They would've killed us both."

He glanced away, trying to hide his pain as he said, "Besides that, my mother had just died. There was no place for me in Akayta, Astrid. In fact, I think the government chose that moment to move in on purpose. My firstborn mother was no longer any kind of barrier to my sentence."

He continued. "So, I went to Velee and soon realized that, even though it's the polar opposite of Akayta, the same type of thing is going on. I began helping different outcasts I found in various ways and soon became pretty well-known among them.

Then I reconnected with Cipher. He'd been committing thefts of everything from jewelry to heavy-duty equipment ever since he'd arrived. His name was associated with criminal activity in Veleen society. He'd become notorious. We talked and continued to disagree.

I didn't hear from him for several months after that. Then I heard from some other people that apparently, "I" had started a tribe for outcasts whose goal was to stop discrimination in Velee and Akayta. It was Cipher. I didn't say anything, and by the time I realized what had happened, it was too late to stop it.

It turns out that Cipher was using my good name to attract people to his "tribe". I've heard different things about the Star through various people I come into contact with, and I highly suspect he's not doing this to just help outcasts. I try to keep an eye on his activities, but that can be hard since I can't get inside. So four months ago, I tried to get in to see what was going on. But he knows me too well and refused. I'm afraid of what he's going to try and do, Astrid." He paused for a few moments.

"Now for the reason why it might be dangerous to be seen with me. I've started a rebellion. Between Cipher and I, the Veleen government is having a hard time making heads or tails of it. So far, at least, they haven't found our base.

Recently, Cipher has been murdering important Veleen political leaders. I don't know why, I don't see what that would gain him."

Astrid tried to process the information. *Cipher is a killer. Knowing him, there must be some kind of morbid, strange logic to it...and now, here is another rebellion. But this time it's the real Rune. But what if it isn't?* She'd fallen for that ploy once and felt uneasy about joining another rebellion, but the moment she looked in Rune's eyes she knew. All uncertainty dissipated.

"Is that where we're going right now?"

"You've got it."

She stopped him once again. "I need you to tell me you aren't going to have me kill anyone," she choked out.

His eyes saddened as they looked at each other. "Never. That's not the way the Cover Rebellion does things."

She nodded, hopes, fears, and so many emotions rushing through her.

"Why were you attending the high commander's speech at the same time I was?" she asked.

"I go to the commander meetings often to keep up on Cipher's movements, and what the Veleens know about the Cover."

"I see."

They swam for a good two hours before a large, tan cluster of rocks came into view. The boulders blended into the surroundings well and were the size of big hills. *I'm guessing that's our destination. I don't see any openings though.* As soon as they reached it, Rune bent down and pressed his hand against the base of the rock. Almost instantly, a large, unseen door parted from the rock and opened.

Astrid stood in shock, staring at what was before her. Mermaids and mermen of all shapes and sizes swam back and forth in an orderly fashion, completing various tasks. The massive, dome-like room had monitors all over the walls and ceilings. Everyone was busy. Some sat stitching together the flexible crimson uniforms of the Cover and others were snapping metal parts together in what looked like stun guns. Many other things were being built, and every individual moved quickly and efficiently. *Stunning.*

The room was hot, and permeated by a tense but determined feeling.

"Welcome to the Cover Rebellion," Rune said grimly as they swam inside and the door closed behind them. Astrid quickly estimated that there were about five hundred merpeople in the room. None of them looked up.

"This is incredible," she replied seriously, her heart pounding. She suddenly realized that she could now truly play a role in ending discrimination on Dalanda.

"Our goal is, like the Star Tribe, to end oppression. But we go about it a different way. We have people from both Akayta and Velee. What we're doing is sending the Akyatans to Velee and the Veleens to Akayta. Then we are slowly but surely infiltrating the government. We can work from there."

Something occurred to Astrid. She turned to Rune with a dubious look.

"This isn't going to mean anything if we don't leave Dalanda. You heard me in Velee, the core is going to explode in just over a week."

He turned away from her. "I know. Come with me. We need to talk about this in private."

She nodded. Astrid examined the passing faces as she swam through the room with Rune. Some people glanced at her and smiled, but most stayed focused on their work. However, one face in particular caught her attention. The man's familiar eyes met hers with recognition.

He left his work and started swimming towards them with a tentative smile. It took a moment for her to recognize the curly orange hair and the face that went with it, but when she did, Astrid gasped. She could feel herself going pale as she clutched Rune's hand.

Astrid's heart sped up. Rune glanced at her with concern when he saw what she was looking at. The approaching merman's face and eyes were different than she remembered. His eyes held deep intelligence and his face was more tanned—the face of someone who'd spent many hours working outside.

He held out his hand, which she shook, trying to force her hands not to tremble. After all, if he was part of the Cover, surely he'd changed since she knew him...she glanced at Rune. *Right?*

"Hello, Astrid," the man said.

She almost choked as an old panic ran through her veins. "H-hello, Dev?"

Dev was one of her old tormentors. Many times she'd be swimming through the streets and he'd corner her, throwing all kinds of insults in her face while beating her up. Once, he almost killed her.

Her breath quickened as she remembered the pain. A few years ago he'd moved to another part of the city. She'd been so relieved. So relieved. There were others that roughed her up frequently, but he was the worst. He hit the hardest and the most often.

And here was this very man standing in front of her. She couldn't hide the fear on her face from Dev's eyes, which immediately deepened with sorrow and intense regret.

"I'm sorry, Astrid. I'm so sorry."

She stared at him. What could she say to this man who had tormented her so much? No malice remained in his eyes, only sincerity.

Anger swept through her for a moment before it was extinguished by fear and shock. Astrid couldn't speak, so she just nodded her head, trying to process what was happening.

"As you know," Rune said rather quietly, "this is Dev. He's one of our pilots."

He glanced at Dev with a questioning look.

"I'll tell her," Dev replied with pain in his eyes.

Rune nodded.

Dev's voice was quiet as he began, "I became the pilot of a mining starship in Akayta several years ago. My parents had two younger children at the time, but after I left, they had a pair of twins as well. The youngest one was a green-and-blue— a five. She was murdered by a one who said she was too "irritating."

I saw it. I saw it, Astrid. The Akaytan government dismissed the situation. That experience shocked me and changed my perspective. I realized just how wrong the caste system was. It was one thing when *I* was terrorizing lower numbers, but it took the shock of the victim being my own sister for me to understand the truth.

I left Akayta and traveled to Velee. Eventually Rune and I ran into each other. After talking and discovering that I wasn't exactly happy living in Velee, Rune invited me here. He decided that my mechanical expertise would be a good thing to have around."

Astrid was shocked, but as she listened to the story and looked at Dev, the war within her eased. Fear and something bordering on hatred gradually ebbed away. She closed her eyes and forced herself to wipe away everything he'd ever done to her. She forced herself to forgive him, even though her emotions were fighting against it. The process would have to be repeated many times, she knew, but the first time is always the hardest.

"I'm glad to see you, Dev," she managed to get out.

He nodded and went back to work, giving her one more sincere, determined, honest smile. So different.

His presence shocked her, but she tried to accept it as they kept moving. When they reached one of the many small rooms that branched out from the main one, Rune turned to face her.

"I've been trying to figure out this melion situation ever since you announced it in Velee. We don't have the resources to build a spacefaring ship, we don't even have blueprints for one." He crossed his arms. "Now, we know where the Veleens have some spaceships, but I want to avoid armed conflict at any cost. Besides there are only four thousand of us, we'd never win."

"So you're willing to avoid conflict at the cost of everything?" she asked quietly. "You know I can't stand the idea of anyone being hurt, but when does it become necessary to try to do something despite the cost? I mean, we would use stun guns, and since that's the case, the only casualties would be on our side. But everyone is going to die anyway if we don't take action."

He shook his head. "This has been occupying my thoughts night and day. I can't think of a good solution. I can't think of a way out." He paused. "Do you remember the conversation we had that day we were caught in the storm?"

She tried to swallow the lump in her throat, "Yes."

"It's like one of those decisions." Anguish filled his eyes.

It was the same anguish that Astrid felt. She put her hand on his arm and sighed. "One step at a time. We need to take this problem one step at a time."

Their eyes locked'.

It was only for a moment, but so many things passed between them. Astrid knew him, she knew her friend. They were struggling together. Through all of it though, was their attachment. The deep connection that she had never felt with Cipher because he wasn't Rune.

He nodded. "Your room number is twenty eighty. The numbers are marked on the doors and you should be able to unlock it since I've entered you into our system now. Dinner is in the main room at nine o'clock."

"Alright."

She bit her lip in worry as she left without another word and found her apartment. Uneasy feelings stirred in her stomach. But she felt something else...something that had always been there, but was only now starting to rise to the surface. Determination. The need to do something. The need to help.

CHAPTER SEVENTEEN

Astrid left, and Rune sat down on a bench running along the wall. His heart was a mix of joy at finally having Astrid back, and twisting emotions about his brother. In explaining to Astrid about Cipher, he'd been forced to remember things he hadn't wanted to— hadn't dared to— face in months. Now that the ball was rolling, it was hard to stop the memories and emotions from flooding back.

He was angry with Cipher, but under that lay pain. He remembered the day Cipher left Akayta. For good.

That day, Rune hovered a short distance outside of Akayta. This was when he usually met Cipher, but his continually wayward brother was late.

That made Rune's stomach turn with fear. If Cipher was late, who knew what had happened to him? Maybe the government caught him. Maybe he was in prison. Cipher was never late. It was uncharacteristic.

Rune searched the horizon anxiously. He hoped his brother hadn't done something irreversible. Ever since Nora was killed, he'd been inching closer and closer to violence and further away from his old, good-natured self. It worried Rune. He didn't want to see his brother cross the line.

There. He saw a form making its way toward him. As soon as he could see it was Cipher, he rushed to him and gave him a brotherly squeeze. Cipher returned it halfheartedly. His hands were clenched in fists, his jaw set in anger.

"What happened?" Rune asked in concern.

Cipher looked away. "I gave a one what he deserved."

"What?"

Cipher looked back at Rune, his eyes burning. "You heard me. I killed a gold. He caught me taking some of his precious possessions and tried to stop me."

Rune's mouth fell open with horror, shock coursing through him.

"He deserved it anyway. He was a friend of the man who murdered Nora. I'm sure he's harmed many red-and-blacks."

"Cipher! Oh, no. You can't...shouldn't...kill people. It's wrong! You know that."

"Not if they hurt me first," Cipher spat.

"This man didn't hurt you— even if he had, it shouldn't make a difference. His friend was the one who killed Nora. You're stooping to their level. Come on, Cipher. You're smarter than that!" Rune shouted. This was what he'd feared. His brother had gone off the edge.

"You're right, I am smart. I'm figuring out how to avoid getting hurt! All of those morals you always talk about don't matter. The ones, in general, have hurt me. I will hurt them back. They're all the same." He gave a dazed laugh that sent chills down Rune's spine.

"Those morals do *matter. You didn't use to be this way. Killing won't gain you anything, you're just going to hurt more people.*

"Keep thinking that way, and you'll keep getting hurt." His eyes flashed with anger, and he stormed away.

"Cipher!" Rune called desperately. *"Cipher!"*

But his brother didn't turn around, and that was the last he saw of him until Velee.

CHAPTER EIGHTEEN

A six-year-old girl sat on the sand, playing with a hand full of pebbles. Curly black hair fell over her shoulders and covered her eyes as she focused intently on making a picture with the stones. He approached her quietly, with a gentle smile on his face. Her tongue was sticking out and it made him want to laugh. The red-and-black mark on her small arm sparkled in the sunlight. His smile faded slightly, he would have to remind her to hide it.

"What're you doing, Nora?" he asked as he slid down beside her.

"I'm building a palace!"

"Really. Who will live there?"

She looked up at him with a quiet intelligence that occasionally surpassed her age.

"Anyone who wants to."

"*Sounds like a good plan to me.*" *He paused.*
"*Nora, you have to cover your mark,*" *he whispered softly.*

She looked at the ground. "But, Cipher...Why should I hide what I am? I can't change it."

He hugged her. "You know why, Nory," he replied firmly.

It was hard enough for him. Hard to put up with the constant hatred and discrimination. But Nora helped him deal with it. If he couldn't protect himself, he could at least protect her.

Cipher left her in front of the house. He glanced back, just in time to see the gold attacking her. He watched her die and he was too late to save her.

CHAPTER NINETEEN

Astrid had barely sat down on the white bed when a small beeping began and steadily sounded. At first she ignored it, thinking it would pass. Astrid tried to focus her thoughts, but the beeping kept interrupting them. *Ugh! What is that sound? I can't concentrate.* She got up and followed the sound.

It was coming from her bag.

Alarmed, she opened it. *It's the silver disk that Effie gave me.* The once completely silver outside was blinking red.

She took it out carefully and opened it. *What's causing this?* she wondered with curiosity. As soon as she unclicked the latch, it popped open.

The message about coordinates fell out...along with the clink of a smaller metal disk.

What? There wasn't a disk in there before. A false bottom. Astrid reached down, picked them up in confusion, and placed them on the bed. Then she looked back into the compact. Two red pieces of palare sat in the very bottom, pressed up against the side. Her heart jumped as she reached in, took them out, and unfolded them.

All sorts of questions rushed through her mind. *Why now? Does this have something to do with what's so important about this disk? Why did Effie give it to me?* She took a deep breath. Foreboding rushed through her in a wave. She began to read her sister's familiar writing,

Dear Astrid. Dear, dear, Astrid. It's hard for me to even write this note, but I know I must. I want you to know, first of all, that I love you very much. You are exceptionally special. I see something in you. You have talent, you have the confidence if you dare to view yourself in the light of being an equal. You hide your strength, you bury it because you don't want to become even more of an outcast. But it is at the center of your character along with compassion. You are a leader. Break the barriers, don't listen to the lies that say you aren't as capable or important as everyone else.

Now for the hard part. I know you are going to have a hard time with this, but you can't let fear control you.

If you are reading this, then I am either dead or in prison. I programmed the compact so that if I don't check

into the program on my computer every forty-eight hours, it will send out a signal and reveal this message to you. Trust me, I won't forget. Don't even think of coming back to Akayta to find out the truth. It's of no use. The reason...

A round tear floated down and landed on the palare as Astrid stared at it, pain etched into every feature of her face as she wept. *Effie. Effie can't be dead. She can't be.* A heavy pressure settled on her chest. Disbelief plunged through her, but then the violent reality hit. *I...I have to keep reading. It's obviously important.* She tried to see through the blur of her tears to grasp the words on the palare. Everything swam as she tried to focus. Finally she could make out her sister's writing again.

The reason I haven't revealed this message to you before is because of the danger of the information it holds. Some people would do anything to obtain it. I hate having to put you in peril by placing it in your possession, but it was in severe danger in Akayta. It's an entirely different level of jeopardy if the information is in your mind. It means that you will constantly be in harm's way, even if you part from this message. This is a last resort. I didn't want to put you in danger, Astrid, but I also know that you are fully capable of handling it.

Now for the actual information. One day, about two years ago, I was reading an old copy of a novel called Time's Grudge...

Astrid's head shot up. *That's the book Honor was reading.* She rooted around in her bag and drew out the book. She'd forgotten that Honor lent it to her. Her eyes flew back to the palare and began reading once more.

I discovered a very complicated code in the text. When you pair that with the actual story in the novel, the code announces that time-travel is possible. There were no specifics about any formulas having to do with time-travel, but the hidden code gave some basic building blocks that helped me discover how it works.

I started experimenting. About two months ago I had a breakthrough and learned more about what I've dubbed "continuance holes." They allow us to travel forward in time up to one hundred years. It turns out that the ability is actually in our very DNA, we just never recognized the purpose of the fixed emarian nanogene.

Continuance holes will only appear in water. I was lucky enough to see a few. What's more, I found a way to calculate when and where they will appear.

I didn't think about the repercussions before I explored it.

A fellow scientist discovered one of my files about the idea. Thankfully it didn't contain any vital information— and I had the other ones locked up, so she couldn't get into them. My computer alerted me she was trying to hack it. Then I realized that just as time-travel could be used for good, it might be used for evil. There is no telling what you can change in the future, or if you can change the past by changing the future. That sounds confusing, but I have reason to wonder.

I wrote down only the most basic information on a single piece of palare and then deleted the results of all my experiments having to do with time-travel. It's better to lose nearly all of my research than for it to be used wrongly.

I've kept quiet and tried to stay out of the other scientists' way. But now I've started receiving threatening messages telling me to hand over my work at appointed places and times. I try to ignore them, but each message is sounding deadlier than the last.

A week ago I received a message from the Akaytan government telling me that I've been reported and must give any information I've been withholding to them. Two days ago they sent a warning and threatened my life. At this moment we are in my apartment and I am staring at you. I know that I have to send you away now. I know that this is going to be dangerous to you. Two factions want this desperately, and you cannot let them have it. It's imperative, Astrid. With this knowledge they could change history to their advantage. No one can know of this information.

What I see as I watch you from across the table is a girl who would speak her mind to the royals. To the very rulers of Akayta. I see an intelligent girl full of ability. You know what you have to do. You know you can't fade into the background of this fight against oppression. It's your fight, and you are meant to take action. Not *necessarily violent action, but action. This is the sister that I know. You don't have to be held back anymore. Go for it.*

Effie

The second sheet of palare held complex mathematical notes and equations involving time-travel, as well as the location of the nanogene. Emotions stirred through her body with ferocity as salty drops fell from her eyes. The world around her seemed so quiet. The silence didn't seem to match the roar of the letter. Its intensity rang with clarity, like a bell within the hurricane of her mind.

With tears still falling, she stood up, determination on her face, then looked back down at the letter full of so much meaning. *A letter that Effie wrote for me.*

She had to figure this out.

There seems to be so much deceit and hatred at play, but I can't let that phase me. It is my duty to find a solution. She continued staring at the message, then looked up again. *It is my duty to protect this knowledge. Effie is right, it's important.*

After carefully putting the letter, false bottom, and message back in the compact, she slipped it into her messenger bag. She swam over to the metal desk. Astrid grabbed a piece of palare and a writing instrument called a rion. Her heart throbbed and her hand trembled for a mere second, but her scientific mind kicked into gear.

She began to form a plan, and the strokes of the rion recorded her thoughts and her knowledge. Her mind could focus on nothing else. Nothing else. This was what was needed of her. Effie believed in her, and that gave Astrid confidence.

As her hand and the ink continued to trace a plan of action, it barely registered that her hunger was growing. Math equations and population estimations permeated every corner of her mind.

Finally, she glanced at the clock and realized that it was already half past nine. *If I want something to eat, I'd better get it now.* She looked back longingly and cautiously at her plans, then at the rion in her hand. This all seemed like a dream, but she knew it wasn't. She continued to grasp the rion, not wanted to let it go. In a strange way, it gave her power. The power to know that she was doing everything she could. The power to know that in one writing tool, she held the ability to make others understand her ideas.

After a few moments, she took a deep breath and stood up. Rolling up her plans firmly, she took them and went out into the curved halls of stone.

CHAPTER TWENTY

Astrid swam to the main room she'd seen first. It was now strangely quiet. Only a few merpeople lingered. Astrid guessed most had returned to their quarters for the night.

The room felt so still. Such a large room filled with nothing but a slight sound every now and then, and cold water.

She went over to a small stand. A sign on it read "Press button and take plate." So she pushed the black button. Sure enough, a hatch in the wall opened, allowing her to take a plate of hot noasé.

After closing the hatch, she surveyed the room for a place to sit. One of the few remaining merpeople was Rune. He sat on a bench along the wall. She swam over and sank down beside him, carefully trying to balance her plate and plans.

He looked up, his face no less intense than earlier.

"Delone kaysha dale," he said in the dialect of language that was specific to Akayta.

She smiled slightly and answered softly, "Lora-tuusone."

It was what they'd always said as a greeting years ago. It was their own special way of saying hello. Technically it meant "may all of your computer terminals function properly" and "may yours as well." It was an old joke. As double digits, by law, they could only own two computer terminals in their lifetime. So they both had been there many times when the other was begging their old one to work. Thus the saying was born.

They sat quietly for a few minutes. Astrid buried herself in her thoughts, figuring out a way to word her next idea to Rune.

She gazed off into the distance, not realizing that Rune was staring at her.

"I know that look. You have an idea and you're trying to figure out how to explain it."

She turned red as she glanced at his tired, but smiling, face. "You're right. Alright…"

She took a deep breath to steady her heartbeat. The plan she was about to propose was risky and she knew it. Astrid sat her plate on the ground and rolled out her palare.

"This plan might work...but I'm not going to lie, it won't be easy. Alright, so you said that they have spaceships in Velee? A friend of mine in Velee mentioned they are sizeable."

"Yes."

"How many are there, and how many people can all of them hold, total?"

He crossed his arms and examined the ceiling while doing the math. He looked back down at her. "There are seventeen total—fifteen large ships, and two smaller ones. They're brand new, barely even been tested. It's part of the government's plan to grow the economy by conducting tours and maybe even founding several off-world colonies. There should be plenty room for all Dalandians, but I'm not sure how we could convince either the Veleens or the Akaytans that they need to get off the planet."

Astrid bit her lip and struggled to continue on. "There are only four thousand of us. We need to find a way to get rid of the security protecting the ships."

"We can send a small advance group to stun them and take over quietly."

Astrid nodded in agreement. "That's what I was thinking."

She pointed to columns on her palare. In each one were numbers and assignments.

"We'll have to get inside and start our ascent before anyone notices, which is going to be the hard part. We also have to know exactly what we're going to do, who's going to pilot the ship, etc. It's not as simple as going in, then flying out free. We'll have to trickle into the building slowly. If someone notices and sounds an alarm, we have to be prepared. We have to have things in place to bar the door and...we have to be equipped with stun guns if it comes down to that. Speed is a vital part of the plan. We also have to alert the Akaytans, Veleens, and, if possible, the Star."

Rune looked at her in despair. "Astrid, it's wild enough just to hope that *we* can make it off the planet in time. We can't try to save everyone— if we do, then we risk dying ourselves in the process."

Tears of pity welled in her eyes. "You once told me not to let that mark hold me back." She took his face in her hands. His eyes stared back at her with sorrow. "Now I'm telling you. Don't let that mark hold you back. Don't let the oppression you've felt because of the mark corrupt your good heart by not forgiving those who've hurt you. You've always been strong, Rune, but I know that, even though you try not to show it, the hatred hurt you too."

Tears were pouring from both of their eyes now. No matter the fact that Rune was perceived as strong, no matter the fact that Astrid wanted to be strong, the scorn poured on them because of that one mark had cut both of them to the heart. Compassion filled her at the sadness she saw in his eyes and understood so well.

"Do you have a plan as to how to get the message to the other tribes?" he asked determinedly.

"Yes...that's the hardest part. In Velee we just need to hack into all of the computer systems, access the monitors, and send the message once we are already ascending. But in Akayta, we have to tell them about the core exploding and the spaceships in Velee *before* we go to the ships, so that they will have time to get there before it happens. Which is risky in itself if they get to Velee quicker than we expected and alert the Veleens about our plan. That would heighten the Veleen security around the ships. One of us has to travel to Akayta to send the message out. We don't have a transmitter strong enough to send a signal from here.

"Then there is the Star Tribe. We can send a message across all of their monitors from here, but we have to time it perfectly. We need to give them just enough time to get to Velee, and board the ships." She looked down at her plan. It included exact times and steps for the warning process.

"It's worth a try," said Rune.

"We don't have much time. Only seven days." It was a statement of fact, but that didn't mean it lacked emotional impact. *Let the pressure commence. There is no room for error here.*

Searing images of her sister flashed through her mind. *Effie. You have to be saved. I know what you said, but I will try my best to help you. I have to go to Akayta anyway. I will not be so close and fail to come after you.* Astrid knew that the possibility of her sister's death was a real one, but she wasn't ready to acknowledge it. *And if there is any chance of her being alive, I want her to survive. I need her to survive.*

~

Effie gritted her teeth. They yanked at her, and she struggled, like most people would. It was to no avail, and Effie knew that, but she had nothing to lose.

Well, that wasn't exactly true. They wanted information about time-travel. Her heart pounded and her throat got tight. *Astrid.*

Effie knew where the information was. The complex equations she hadn't been able to commit to memory.

With Astrid.

She wanted to kick herself. She should never have given it to her. They would go after her sister if they found out.

They will kill Astrid.

Her resolve steeled as the palace police roughly hauled her into the imperial prison building. The cold metal of a cell door swished through the water. For Astrid, she would endure whatever they had in store for her. For Astrid, she would hold her tongue, no matter the cost.

For Astrid.

CHAPTER TWENTY-ONE

Astrid peered up at the bright sun. Rune sat beside her, reading a novel out loud.

"Alton looked over at Sapphire and smiled, 'You're so wonderful, Sapphire. You always care about others more than yourself.'

Sapphire smiled back and said, 'You're pretty nice also.' Sapphire felt her face go red. He leaned over and kissed her. Sapphire had never felt so wonderful in all of her life.

As he drew back, touched her cheek, and looked into her blue eyes he said, 'I love you so much, Sapphire. You are so amazing and beautiful.'

'I love you too,' she whispered.

Then they kissed."

Rune set the book down and looked up at Astrid, his eyes laughing.

"I know that's supposed to be a serious moment, but it just strikes me as amusing instead. Surely they could've said something better than, 'You're amazing and beautiful...I love you.' It's much too vague. He might as well have said, 'You like noasé and I like noasé. We're made for each other,'" he said in a deadpan voice.

Astrid laughed so hard her stomach hurt. Finally she choked out, "Yes. Surely they could've said something a little deeper like, 'I love the feeling of your hand in mine. I've struggled with my feelings knowing that we could never be together, but now we can.' That would have been much less cheesy."

"'I love the feeling of your hand in mine?'" He was just barely keeping his smile from bursting into full-fledged grin. "Deeper?"

Astrid grinned. "Yes. Absolutely!"

"But, 'I love the feeling of your hand in mine?'" he asked again, his grin breaking loose.

"Alright, alright. Writing isn't my strong suit! What can you come up with?" she asked playfully, raising her eyebrows in challenge.

"Hmm, what about... 'Within this world of darkness, you give me a light. I desperately need you. You've shown me that darkness can be defeated. It's not everlasting, and it won't continue to reside in me if I push it out. You've made me a better person.'"

She looked thoughtful for a second, "I will admit that's much better, but it's still..."

He gave an exaggerated sigh. "How about this?" He took a breath and then proceeded to rush through everything he'd already said. "Within a world of darkness, you give me a light. I need you. You've shown me that I can defeat the darkness. I can push it out. You've made me a better person...I love the feeling of your hand in mine.""

Astrid burst into laughter, "Much better. Maybe you should become an author...you have that...poetic streak to you."

"You think so?" he asked, raising his eyebrows with a grin.

"All I can say is that you wrote that scene much better than the author did."

They both sat there laughing for quite some time.

Astrid slept through the night restlessly, waking up every hour or so. Even the calming dream didn't help very much. The high commander's death bothered her. It kept playing over and over in her head. There was another reason Cipher was carrying out his plan...other than what he'd told her. There was more to it. Something was very wrong, but she didn't know what and she couldn't guess.

Finally she got up, changed into one of the dark red, Cover Rebellion shirts, and brushed her hair. After pulling it into a side ponytail, she brushed away the salt that had gathered on her tail overnight.

As she looked in the mirror, she realized that today was her birthday. *I'm seventeen. So much has changed. Another year older.* She stared at her reflection for a couple of minutes thinking of all the things she'd experienced in life, and what she had yet to experience. There were so many things she was grateful for, and so many things she had yet to do.

Astrid left the mirror, sat on the bed, and forced herself to think through the plan day by day. She sat clutching the precious compact that held such unique knowledge. Today was a day of training. A day of practicing, and everyone learning their parts in the plan.

She filed into the main room with the other merpeople. The room was ripe with tension. Everyone could sense that something major was happening. They'd all been summoned on their devices for the assembly that morning.

Ten minutes later, Rune swam above the rest of them and, after glancing around, began to speak, "As some of you have heard, the cadence of the melions is off, and Dalanda will explode in only six days. Therefore, we must evacuate the planet. Astrid, our newest member and trusted friend, has come up with a plan. I'll let her explain."

She gulped with worry as she swam up next to him. Looking out over the cluster of faces made her heart beat faster than it should have. *Public speaking is not part of my skill set. It's alright though. I have to do this.* She stuttered at first as she showed her plans and began to explain, but after a few moments she fell into a rhythm. She barely saw the serious, concentrated faces of the outcasts anymore as she poured herself into relating her ideas through words. She told of the plan, and also of the schedule. Finally she finished and recalled her audience. Silence filled the water.

The different expressions reflected the feelings that pervaded the water. Tension. Anxiety. Hope. Fear. Love. Foreboding. Hurt. Nobody knew what to say, but they knew what they had to do.

"Like Astrid said, we'll begin training today. If you look on your handheld devices you'll see that you have been assigned to a group and a specific task. You'll practice your tasks today. Everything depends on exact timing. You can't be five minutes late or early pushing a button, or setting out to travel. Let's get started."

Astrid swam back down into the comforting mass of confident people who were dispersing to work on their assigned tasks. Among them she felt invisible, which, as strange as it may seem, reminded her of home. Of Effie's comfort. She closed her eyes. She would soon know Effie's fate. Despite what her sister said, she had to go after her, and it was on her way anyways. Uneasiness for Effie ticked like a clock inside her bones.

A sharp beeping sound drew her attention to her tablet. A screen popped up telling her the task she'd been assigned and detailing timing, even though she had it memorized. She and Rune had taken most of the previous night to assign everyone tasks according to their strong suits.

She watched all of the action. One mermaid with a bright green tail was firing a stun gun at a target. It beeped twice telling her that she'd hit dead center. The grey cave was full of collective hope. Desperate longing. Everyone aching for a better world. Everyone wishing to succeed.

Her heart rose with the inspiration of possibility.

~

Astrid glanced at a timepiece on the wall. *Only one hour until I set out.* It was time to rescue Effie and send the message. Time had gone quickly because she was caught in a never ending stream of planning and adjusting plans.

She quickly ate, then gathered supplies. The hour flew by with ferocity. Finally she was at the door, a bag over her shoulder. Tucked safely within it was the compact. Astrid hadn't told Rune about Effie's note yet. It wasn't that she didn't trust him, it was the fact that she didn't want to put him in danger. It was her personal mission. She would see her sister safe.

"I'll see you soon," he said, nodding at her grimly. With that, the big stone door closed with a scrape.

Astrid was once more completely alone in the vastness of the planet.

CHAPTER TWENTY-TWO

The voice coming through the communication device was clear and sharp, "We've tortured the prisoner, we've tried to bribe her, but she won't tell us anything."

Cipher growled in frustration. If he was able to time-travel, he would know things no one else did. He could change history. The desire held him firmly in its grip. He already had power, but he wanted more. He wanted to control any element that might give him leverage, another tool in achieving his deepest wishes. The Akaytans wouldn't have told him about it in the first place, but he had informants. They would have to learn they couldn't trick him.

"So torture her more. She has to give in eventually. You've searched her computer, her home, everything, correct?" Cipher asked into the communication device.

"Of course we've searched everything, sir," the voice replied begrudgingly. The man continued offhandedly, "As for torturing the prisoner, we've put her through the worst kinds we have, but she's stubborn. I don't think it will help to do any more. I guess being a troublemaker runs in the family. Just a few weeks ago her sister escaped off to who knows where right before being arrested. She'd been doing illegal experiments and was going off about the end of the world. We gave the prisoner a harsh warning after she helped her sibling escape, but that's all. She's a firstborn after all. It's a pity that she's stooped to her sister's level. A red-and-black. I can't even imagine." Disgust trickled through his voice.

Of course you can't, you're too busy abusing us, Cipher thought with bitterness. His Akaytan contacts knew nothing about his origins. All they needed to know was that he should be feared.

Then he froze in his seat as he realized the rest of what the man had said. End of the world...a few weeks ago... a red-and-black leaving Akayta. Suddenly the pieces clicked. *Astrid. Astrid's sister is the one who knows about time-travel.*

He suddenly knew where that information was. *Astrid has it.*

But how? She'd only brought a few basic things with her when she'd come to the Star. Or Rune brought her...but he didn't want to admit that to himself. She hadn't come of her own will, she ran away, and now she was with his brother. He cringed. He thought Astrid would understand his reasoning, but she didn't. Anger crashed through his heart uncontrollably.

Anyway, he'd checked her messenger bag himself. It only contained a coordinate director, a strange compact, a...wait, the compact, it must have contained something other than what he'd seen. *That's the only explanation I have.* He was sure that Astrid's sister wouldn't have completely destroyed her findings, and none of them were in Akayta. That left only one option. Astrid and the compact.

"Alright, then," he whispered through clenched teeth.

The communication device went silent, the person on the other end waiting for him to say something.

"Don't torture the girl anymore. In fact, don't concern yourself with this matter any longer."

"What?" The man sounded surprised.

"Goodbye," Cipher replied as he ended the call. He pressed the buttons that would connect him with the two scouts tracking Astrid. He'd sent them to follow her from the moment she left. Cipher wasn't stupid. He didn't want to lose her and, unfortunately, his instincts proved correct.

She abandoned me and now she has something I need.

He would do anything it took to get that tool. Time-travel? The possibilities were endless.

His gaze brimmed with ire as his call was answered.

"Hello?"

He paused. Hesitation stopped him for a moment, but then he made his decision. The desire for control overruled everything else.

"Move in on your object. She has a silver compact that contains important pieces of military information. Do whatever you must— just get the compact."

He ended the call and crossed his arms. He wanted Astrid to love him, but he wanted power more.

CHAPTER TWENTY-THREE

Astrid dug out a coordinate director and set it for Akayta. Then, staring at the waving blue ocean in front of her, she set off.

It was lonely as she swam along at a steady pace, but she was used to that. Her mind swirled around time-travel, Effie, Rune, and Honor. Finally, it came to rest on Cipher.

Pity filled her heart. He could have been a good man, she knew it. But he decided to take revenge instead. *I still don't know what his plan is. There is more to it than it seems.* That thought made her uncomfortable. There was a missing piece, and she knew it was somehow vital.

Cipher's face flashed through her mind, provoking her curiosity about his earlier years. She remembered what Rune said to him in the video. *"I know that you won't harm Astrid because of the soft spot you've always had for her. I believe it's the only soft spot in that cold heart of yours."*

Astrid remembered the crashing emotions that had come upon her when she heard Cipher's views on the world. Even though she now knew it hadn't been Rune, it still affected her. The fact that someone could truthfully believe that way. *Maybe the thing that scares me is that I can understand how he would arrive at that position. It just reminds me not to let myself slip.*

The hours passed tiredly at she continued swimming. She thought she felt strange waves running through the water...almost like an earthquake. *The core really is going to explode. I just hope these people listen to us.* She glanced at her timepiece, *One hour until I reach Akayta.* Time felt like it was running through her body and slipping through her fingers like liquid. She couldn't control it, and it was running away from her. She quickened her pace.

At that moment she felt something in the water...like an inaudible sound. A vibration. She whipped around. As soon as she did, arms encircled her neck with the intent of choking her. The bag slung over her arm was yanked. *No. The compact!* She bent her elbow to try and keep the bag from falling into her attackers' hands. *Can't breathe...* Her water supply was cut off as she tried to force the hands off her throat with her own.

Then she remembered something. *Maybe Cipher's training will come in handy after all.* She took one short moment to steady herself, then she dropped, yanking herself from her attackers' grasp at an angle and rolling away, the bag still in her possession. She faced them, sucking in deep gulps of water, her eyes showing her panic. She didn't feel prepared for this, but then again, who would?

Astrid barely caught a glimpse of the two, masked figures before they rushed her again. She flipped then used that momentum to barrel into their stomachs, making them stumble. Then she fled. Not even glancing back, she darted away as fast as she possibly could. Her heart pounded and her adrenaline rushed. She knew that the slight stumble she caused them would only last for a few seconds. *Please.* Her hand tightened even more around the string of her bag as she looked back. They were already in pursuit.

Up on the right rose a tall, waving kelp forest. Just what she needed. She dove into the mass of green, swaying stalks. Astrid looked up and could see nothing but kelp, just like in front of her. *They won't be able to swim overhead and spot me.* She drew breaths rapidly as she plunged easily through the plants, their soft leaves brushing against her in a comforting, quieting way.

She paused after a few minutes, letting the quiet, mysterious vegetation settle around her. There were no noises that indicated the continuation of the pursuit. They wouldn't be able to find her in this vast forest. Her breathing evened out, and her heart slowed. It was darker here than out in the sunlight, but she could still make out the deep green colors around her.

Something squishy brushed past her arm and she jumped. Her mouth changed into a smile.

It was a pleddy. The animal moved slowly as she sat down to watch it. She needed to rest anyway. The brownish-gold head sparkled with scales, and its wide fish eyes didn't blink. Instead of its head closing off in a neck, the sides continued, changing from scales to a smooth substance with seven tentacles. The translucent bits lit up with every color imaginable, and the colors pulsed like they themselves were the animal's heart.

Astrid had scared away most animals when she burst into their forest home, but now they were coming out again since she was sitting still. Fish of all sorts swam over her head. The volume of life and color and quiet made her smile.

She spotted a group of tiny fish. Five could fit in her hands at once. They lit up with a pulsing golden color. Lightning fish. She and Rune used to go to another kelp forest near Akayta to catch them. The fish darted fast, which made them a challenge to catch, then they would always release them after they were done. She sighed with contentment and closed her eyes. Astrid knew she had to keep moving, so she reluctantly got up and used her coordinate director to guide her out of the forest and into Akayta.

Her temporary contentment was soon gone, replaced with the urgency and fear pulling her back toward her torturous home. She kept a close, weary watch on her surroundings as she continued on, securely tying the string of her bag to her arm instead of just carrying it. *I have to make it to Akayta so I can warn them, and I can't let this compact fall into anyone else's hands.*

Astrid nearly cried when the lights of Akayta came into view. She had experienced so many bad things there, and she had no wish to visit again, but she had to plant the transmitter to deliver the message.

More importantly, she had to discover Effie's fate.

Astrid glanced down at the bag that held the compact and untied it from her arm. She donned a hooded black cape. She pulled the hood over her head. It obscured her face. With that, she hid the bag under her cape, took a deep breath, and entered Akayta.

CHAPTER TWENTY-FOUR

Unfortunately I know where to start. The Imperial Prison. If Effie is anywhere, she's there. Astrid's heart quickened as she made her way through the back alleys, avoiding any public places with cameras. She only had a loose plan, and she knew it was risky, but she desperately needed to know.

Finally she reached the gate that led into the prison. She stared at them from across the street wondering how to get in. *There has to be some way,* she thought as she watched the guard swim back and forth. The building that held the cells was a medium-sized, square, white brick structure. It was covered by a clear dome. She would have to disable the cameras inside.

The black gate was the only entrance, and it was guarded by a disgruntled merman. *Well, a distraction might work. What do I have that could draw his attention elsewhere?* She snapped her fingers. Astrid knew exactly what to do, but she had to be careful. She took the transmitter she'd rigged to send the message out of her bag and quickly programmed another instruction. She carefully hit send on her new program, double-checking to be sure it wasn't the message. Water seemed to ignore her lungs in the few minutes she waited. Then it happened.

"Robbery!" came a shrieking shout from a speaker just around the corner. The guard perked up and left his post.

Yes. Astrid had programmed one of the speakers that was stationed throughout the city so they couldn't trace the signal back to her. It was just the distraction she needed, and they wouldn't be able to make heads or tails of it.

The guard might return any moment. She dashed toward the unwatched gate, cracked it enough to slip inside, then closed it once more.

She darted around to the back alley and found a round, metal structure sticking out of the wall. It controlled the technological elements of the block. A tangle of wires covered its surface, and it was obvious it hadn't been touched for quite a while. She found the wires that directed the cameras and their control box. She managed to set them all on a loop. That would hopefully protect her for a while...if she hadn't already been seen. Technology, probably the one thing she loved more than geology.

She went back around to the front and slipped through the door to the prison. Astrid sped silently through the narrow grey halls, glancing left and right at any occupants the cells carried. There weren't very many. *Please be here!* She turned a corner and continued searching. The prisoners gazed at her blankly. Sickly groans were the only sounds to be heard. She went up and down the different corridors, searching for her sister, her heart speeding at the thought that a guard could catch her at any moment.

Then Astrid saw Effie. She froze. Relief, and then fear for Effie's well-being rushed into her simultaneously. Her sister was sitting in the corner of the grey stone cell, her intelligent eyes staring into the distance. Her fine, black hair was in a state of disarray, and her mouth set in a thin line.

"Effie?" Her voice cracked.

Her sister's head whipped around, keen eyes squinting. "Astrid? Is that you?" Her voice was filled with surprise and displeasure. She slowly swam to the bars. Astrid noticed she was having trouble moving. Effie's face twisted in pain.

"I told you not to come. It's dangerous." Her face reflected disbelief and worry as she glanced past Astrid, trying to see if a guard was coming.

"It was on my way. Besides, I couldn't leave you. You knew that."

"I can't go with you, Astrid." Effie bit her lip as she gestured to her tail. "They've...they've been torturing me, trying to get the time-travel formulas out of me."

Astrid gasped.

"They've injured me. I can't swim without overwhelming pain."

No. I have to get her out. Astrid's emotions swirled. Seeing her sister trapped in such a vulnerable position made her want to cry. She glanced down the hall. *There's no telling how much time we have before the guard is back at his station.*

"I'll help you. We just have to get you out of this cell!"

Effie's eyes pierced Astrid's. "No. Don't risk yourself."

Astrid just shook her head, tearing her gaze from her sister's and looking at the lock. It was a number pad. She moved with the speed she knew was necessary as she took a rectangular device out of her bag and attached it to the keypad.

Within moments she discovered the combination. Her heart pounded, making it harder to breathe as she waited for the door to click open. The ping sounded through the air when the latch opened. *I hope no one heard that.* Astrid immediately rushed in and hugged her sister. Effie hugged her back, but the tension was evident. She was truly worried about her, and all her nerves were on edge. *She's just as concerned about me,* Astrid realized.

"How can you help me? I'll only slow you down and cause us both to be captured," Effie said, hopelessness resounding through her voice.

"Come on! You have to make an effort. I thought about what might happen if you were injured, so I brought a medical supply kit. Here. Hurry."

She pulled out a small box, and handed Effie a pill for pain. Then she gave her a black, hooded cloak, which she donned.

Astrid held out her hand to her injured sister. Their eyes met and Effie grasped her sister's hand tightly with love.

"It's going to be okay," Astrid said.

The pair of sisters stole down the hall, Astrid struggling to support Effie. They halted and relief flooded through her when she saw that the sentry was down the street, talking casually with a friend, his back turned to them. Then they plunged on as quietly as possible and left the gate.

The area around the prison was scarce of merpeople, which made Astrid nervous, as they were more likely to be noticed. She let out a breath as she tried to support Effie, whose face twisted with pain. Every bone inside Astrid urged her forward, telling her that speed was of the essence. The danger was obvious. As they swam into more populated areas, most people didn't even give them a second glance.

Astrid was getting tired, and the shoulder she was using to support Effie felt like it was on fire. *Almost to the edge of town.*

At that moment, a distant volley of cries rose into the water causing Astrid to glance back, and her heart to beat more quickly.

"They've discovered you're gone. We have to move faster," said Astrid, adrenaline coursing through her.

They sped through Akayta at the quickest pace they could manage. Her world seemed to consist of panting, aching, and the uproar behind them.

By the time they crossed the Akaytan border, the uproar could no longer be heard. *It's time to plant the transmitter.*

Astrid glanced at her sister as she stopped, "Just a second. I have to do something. I'll explain later."

She dug into her bag and pulled out the device that was rigged to send the message. She bent down, burying it in the sand so it wouldn't be seen. It would transmit the message at just the right time so that the Akaytans would be able to reach the ships in Velee, and takeoff before the explosion.

All the while, fear nagged at her. Were they being pursued by the Akaytan officials? What about the two attackers from earlier?

It took a moment for her to realize that it was done. That her job in Akayta was done forever. She put her sister's arm around her neck and they started off.

Astrid never looked back.

CHAPTER TWENTY-FIVE

"So that's what has happened since I left," finished Astrid as she swam with Effie.

They were nearing the Cover base, and she was relieved. Every moment of the trip back she'd been on the lookout for attackers. She'd stayed up most of the night on watch. Astrid glanced at her timepiece. *I seem to be doing that every few minutes.* She had a new awareness of the short time left before the explosion of the core. The tension was building inside her.

"I told you you're special," said Effie with a grin.

"Well, I don't feel quite so helpless anymore," she replied with a small smile. *Though I'm still lonely in a strange way.*

The rock base came into view. "Only three days until we set our plan into action," she said with a sigh.

When they arrived, Astrid bent down and pushed the base of the rock to open the door.

The flurry of activity that met them inside was frantic. Noise filled the dome as various groups trained and rehearsed signals over and over again. Voices permeated the water, instructing, commanding, and answering. Every noise echoed back and forth in the big room.

One person would miss their laser gun target, then another and another. One person would hit dead center, then another and another.

Astrid searched the room for Rune. She spotted him sitting in a corner, observing the activity closely. She made her way over to him with Effie.

He stood up and looked at her sister with confusion.

"Who's this?"

"Effie, my sister," she replied.

Understanding lit up his face. "I remember you talking about her." He held out his hand and she shook it. "Welcome."

"What's her number? I want to take her to her room now. It's been a very long journey for us."

Effie was silent. Amusement glinted in her eyes.

"Twenty eighty-one," he answered.

"I'll be back soon." With that Astrid turned away and helped Effie to her room.

Once they were inside and seated on the bed Effie said, "You seem entirely comfortable with him. Or am I wrong?" She grinned.

Astrid blushed, "I know him."

"Who is he?"

"Rune," she replied quietly.

Understanding and amazement dawned upon Effie's face. She had comforted Astrid many times after Rune's departure.

Astrid paused for a moment. "How's your tail?"

Effie's smile fell. "It hurts, that's for sure, but not very much when I don't move."

Astrid stood up, "I'll get doctor to come see you. Are you going to be alright?"

Effie's eye softened. "I'll be fine. I'm very proud of you, Astrid. You're a very brave and true-hearted individual."

Astrid smiled and closed the door softly. *I don't feel brave,* she thought with a sigh. She headed back to the main room, then sat down by Rune.

"How is it going?" she asked. Strangely, even though she still had that fear in her— that desire to crawl into a corner and hide, or collapse because of all her emotions— she felt a duty pushing her to take initiative. A responsibility to help people. That's what kept her from doing nothing, however much she was being pushed into the ground by the forces acting against her.

She was brought out of her thoughts by Rune's voice replying, "Everyone is working hard. We haven't had much time, but they're doing the best they can. Were you successful?"

"Yes. The message is sent." She looked at him. "Only three days."

"I know."

CHAPTER TWENTY-SIX

Having Effie under the same roof had a calming effect on Astrid. She spent as much time with her as possible, but the hurricane was coming and she had a job to do. A sense of purpose she never thought she would get the chance to experience. All the while, the clock steadily ticked down.

The day she'd feared for so many weeks arrived. Astrid and Rune checked supplies, timing, and everything else. Finally, Rune called an assembly. It was half an hour before the troupe was scheduled to set out for Velee. He took Astrid's hand and guided her up above the crowd with him. He faced the Cover.

"We are about to set out on a vital mission which our lives depend on. I've watched you all working hard to practice for your missions the last couple of days. If you keep up that hard work, we'll succeed. This isn't the time to relax. It's the time to push harder than ever— the one last push to reach our goal."

His strong voice rang through the cavern. It was a voice that Astrid would listen to. It held power and confidence. Not forced or insincere, but strong and convicted.

Rune continued, "The only part of the mission we haven't discussed yet is the signal for our ship to liftoff." He glanced at Astrid. They had talked about it earlier. "The person who is going to flip that switch will have monitors showing every area of the ship and outside of it. When you see this signal," he paused, holding his right fist straight up in the air, "you are to start the ascent of the ship. There are only two people that you take that order from. Astrid or I."

Astrid looked up in surprise at this. *Me?*

"We'll depart in twenty-five minutes. Be ready." With that they swam down, and the last bout of frenzied activity began.

Rune took her hand. "I was thinking that if one of us dies, there will be someone else to take charge. Besides, you're perfectly capable and this is your plan. You may see something that I don't. My mind doesn't work quite like yours."

She smiled slightly, but was still shocked. "Alright."

He held her eyes for a moment and whispered, "We can do this, Astrid," in a voice that betrayed his own fright.

She took his hand. "We *will* do this."

It felt like only five minutes passed before the group set out. Astrid glanced toward her sister as the big stone door shut for the last time. Two merpeople were carrying her. The water seemed cold as she looked at the time, then the people around her. It would take them two hours to get to the ships. From that point on, it would only be three hours until the core exploded. *We only have one shot at this. One chance to get off the planet in time. It all depends on every single person doing their job on time.*

The closer they got to Velee, the harder her heart pounded. There was also the risk of early discovery. The outline of the city rose on the horizon.

"Halt," called Rune.

It was loud in Astrid's ears since she was hovering next to him.

"You all know what to do. Split into small groups of twos and threes and gradually make your way to the shiphouse. Those of you assigned as the advance group to take out the guards, hurry ahead."

People started carrying out their orders. Slowly, different sets spread away in the distance as they skirted the city in a small but steady stream. The shiphouse was at the edge of the city and, from what she'd heard, it was huge. She stayed with Rune as the headed towards Velee.

Her timepiece seemed to be her only interaction with the world. Everything seemed silent to her, even as she passed nervously through the crowded marketplace. The only thing that changed was the time that showed on her timepiece. It was the center of the world. Moments, minutes, and hours flying away without so much as slowing down to look back.

The shiphouse came into sight. Yesterday she'd seen a picture of the domed building. It spread much further than she could have imagined. Once the ships were ready to ascend, the top of the the dome would be lifted mechanically by the push of a button. That would take approximately three minutes. Then all of Velee would know their intentions. From that point they would have only a short time to send the message to the Veleens and the Star tribe, and start the Cover ship's liftoff before they realized what was happening.

When they reached the edifice, the Cover guard nodded at them with recognition and cracked the great metal door, allowing them to enter. Her eyes watched the single guard until the closing door cut off her line of sight. *That means the Veleen guards have been captured,* she thought in surprise. Astrid had half-expected to swim into a battlefield.

At first sight, everything appeared normal in the impressive bay that held the spaceships. She quickly estimated the number of Cover already present. She and Rune had purposely been in the last group to trickle in. *They're all here.*

The looks on their faces were strange and rigid and they were barely moving. *They should be bustling to their stations.* Foreboding filled her body and she felt like she could barely breathe. Glancing at Rune, she saw that he sensed the same thing. It was like the silent moment before a predator seizes his prey.

CHAPTER TWENTY-SEVEN

"Hands in the open!" came a rough voice from behind Astrid and Rune. Panic coursed through her as she brought her empty hands up into the open water. *No. We've barely begun and we've already been discovered. They have to listen to us. We have to leave the planet.* She felt herself trembling as the voice told them to line up against the wall.

The uniforms. The faces. She knew them. They weren't the Veleens, as she'd anticipated. They were the Star. *No.* The familiar faces, many of them with kind eyes, made her feel like crumbling. But she didn't have the time or the option to break down.

Astrid and Rune joined the other members of the Cover who were looking to their leaders for reassurance and direction. Her mind raced. She wasn't sure what to do. Her eyes fell on those of the man who'd captured them, then ran to the gun trained on her. *We have to do something.* More of the Cover slowly emerged from behind the ships. Every single one was armed. She felt the presence of the stun gun she'd been given hidden in a holster under her long shirt. Each member of the Cover carried one. Surrounded. It was a silent standoff. She noticed that hers weren't the only hands shaking. Many of the Cover looked unsure. Vulnerable.

That gave her an idea. Maybe it was a futile one, but at this point, with the clock ticking down, she decided it was worth a try.

"Attack!" she yelled, her hand shaking as she whipped out her stun gun and stunned the enemy merman in front of her. The other members of the Cover, including Rune, didn't hesitate at her command. The feeling of disabling someone wasn't good, even if it was necessary. *It's still violence.* Her stomach turned, but the adrenaline rush took over. She turned and began aiming at the enemies, who could be identified by their black Star uniforms. All of the Cover wore the crimson color. Lasers cut through the water with their light as both stun lasers and lethal lasers rang back and forth. It reminded Astrid of the battle in the Star complex. Her heart rose slightly as she saw that the Cover were easily winning.

At that moment she heard a call ring out from one of the enemy.

"Reinforcements convene!"

Adrenaline coursed through her. *No! We can't hold out against more.*

A stream of a hundred or so rushed in.

Every person she shot with her stun gun made her wince. To put someone else in pain... Whatever their stories, they were still people. Whatever their faults, they were still people. Some of them good, like Honor and Ris. She ducked back and forth and found herself using moves Cipher had taught her. Sound after sound, second after second, face after face. Something lingered on the edge of her mind, but she couldn't quite grasp it.

Then, just as she was about to shoot, she realized the face opposite her was one she recognized. The eyes met hers and lit with realization. Ris's hand held fast, but she didn't shoot.

"Ris!"

"You're with them, Astrid?" Her face paled.

They both panted as they faced each other in battle. What they were supposed to do was shoot each other. But how could they? But what if one did. They were friends, right? These thoughts spun through the minds of both Astrid and Ris.

This is the dilemma Rune and I talked about. This is civil war.

"They're right, Ris. Star is a lie. It isn't real. Rune has ulterior motives. He isn't even the real Rune. His name is Cipher."

"No...no," said Ris as they stood there, guns trained on each other and battle raging around them. The two friends who were now supposed to be enemies. In their hearts they knew they could not be, but in the physical realm it was their duty. Loyalty to faction? Or loyalty to friend? Loyalty to belief? Or loyalty to the ones you've established a trust with? The fighting continued around them, but they just stood there, trying to figure out their next move.

"It *is* true," Astrid whispered. "Rune's paradise may not be real, but I'm sure there is something similar out there. I'm sure we all can find it."

"You saved me once and you're my friend. I can't kill you." With that Ris threw down her gun and with one last look fled, weaving in and out of the flurried motion.

Astrid wanted to follow, but she didn't have time, another person was already attacking her. She stunned him. A new question rose and flashed through her mind. *How did the Star know that we would be here? Our message wouldn't have reached them in time for them to beat us here.* She dismissed it. A figure entered the fray. The form was familiar and sent shivers through her body.

"Cease fire," a voice yelled. The fire of both sides faltered because no one could clearly identify who was speaking.

"Cease fire," came the voice once more.

Astrid couldn't quite make him out through all the dust and sand in the water.

She found herself next to Rune as he, in turn, shouted, "Cease fire."

All of the merpeople on both sides stared unsurely at the figure making his way through the cloud of dirt. Rune's face darkened as he took Astrid's hand and they made their way to the front to meet the figure. Everything and everyone was on edge. She clutched her stun gun, ready to raise it again if necessary. Taking a look around as she swam with Rune, her heart rose into her throat as she saw dozens of bodies strewn on the ground. It was hard to distinguish through the white dust whether they were stunned Star or dead Cover.

The figure neared and Astrid saw his face. She wasn't surprised, after all it did make sense that he would be here. It still shook her though. Being shaken and surprised are not the same thing. Being shaken is much worse.

Cipher's face was grim, there wasn't even a hint of a sadistic smile or triumphant grin. His eyes were completely serious, and almost deadly. "We're in this position once more, but this time it has gone beyond our words and manifested into physical violence. Perhaps we can come to a truce if we talk." He looked straight at Rune as he said this, then nodded with his head towards an area of the shiphouse where neither the Star nor the Cover would be able to hear.

Rune gave a sharp nod. His hand still held Astrid's. What people saw if they looked at him in that moment was a strong, determined, sharp-witted leader. What Astrid could feel in his hand was a peaceful boy who loved his brother and needed support.

Cipher made his way to the barren spot that was partially hidden from view by a spacecraft. As Rune followed him, Astrid whispered, "I'm coming with you."

He barely acknowledged it, but she knew he heard.

The silence when they reached the speaking area was rigid. Cipher hovered there with his back to them and his hands clasped tightly behind it. He turned, his steel gaze stealing any attention away from his nervousness.

"You're a coward," he said.

Rune stared at him with tired sadness. "And you're a cheat."

"That may be, but I'm doing it for the right reasons."

"What right reasons?" asked Astrid quietly, drawing Cipher's gaze and a look of pain. She was uncomfortable, but not enough to keep from speaking the truth.

"I do have reasons, Astrid. Reasons I thought you understood." His voice was iron as he looked at her, trying to hide his inner misery.

Her voice escalated with pity and pain. "I don't understand cruelty being used as a tool of justice. It won't be justice anymore by the time you're done with it. You don't have to stoop to that level. You don't have to be a killer, Cipher!" Cipher wasn't Rune, but he was someone she'd come to know, despite the lie about his identity.

"If we're name-calling, then you're a deserter. You have no loyalty," he said coldly, his voice raised.

Anger boiled to the surface as she shouted back, "I never pledged loyalty to a person who trains assassins and yet hides when the battle starts! The facade of peace was a lie. Why would you expect me to believe anything you say?"

"As far as I'm concerned, you're the one who lied! You came in and pretended goodwill…"

"Leave her alone! This is my battle. She shouldn't have to suffer for it," Rune shouted, even louder than his brother. Up to this point he had been mostly quiet, the storm brewing within him. His brother had stolen his identity, become a murderer— yet he was being contentious, like he had some kind of right.

Cipher's gaze shifted back to Rune's and his eyes darkened with bitterness. "This became her battle when she abandoned me."

"She never hurt you. You know that the only person hurt was me, when I had to entrust her care to you."

"What makes you think that you were in a more dire position than her, while she was lying in my hospital dying from Veleen poison that you failed to protect her from?" Cipher replied angrily.

"If you care enough to listen, my worry was for her well-being. Your heart has turned so cold that you ignore me every time I try to reach out. I don't trust you with piece of kelp anymore, yet I had to trust you with her in order to save her life."

"You always think you're better than me. But you have no idea how untrue that is," Cipher spouted vehemently.

"You are my brother! Remember how close we used to be? I know you inside and out, or at least I used to. Your have no excuse for your actions."

"What do you know of me now? I am different. I won't be pushed around by the desires and thoughts of people who refuse to grow. The Akaytans did enough to me, and I allowed them to. I'm turning their own wave of hate against them. There is no doubt that I will make them taste their own hostility. They will suffer as I did. I'm bringing change, and everyone knows it. I don't hide it. But you— you cower under my shadow, hoping to bring change without anyone seeing you. You are a coward."

Being called a coward made Rune angry, but it also hurt. Cipher was still his brother. As much as he wanted to get away from him, away from the attachment...they were forever bound by bonds of brotherhood.

Yet they were enemies. No confidence existed between them any longer. Their trust had completely disintegrated.

Rune stared at him. "You won't break through my barriers by prodding me. I'm doing what I think is right. Besides, I don't turn my anger into violence. Revenge is never honorable, no matter how much you want to repay the wrongs inflicted on you.

"If you want to talk about hiding, then what about you hiding your plans from your own people? That's selfish. If they don't know your goals, then you're committing them all to fighting, and possibly dying, for something they don't believe in— and something that will be lost if you die. You are misleading and using them."

"I'm giving them a world where they will be treated with respect. Besides, they trust me implicitly. And trust is so important, right?" he asked mockingly.

"They trust *my* name! A trust you haven't earned. Face the fact that you're a thief and murderer. You've become the oppressor or, if you haven't already, you're about to."

Cipher stood tall, his eyes burning with bitterness and strong hatred. "You can't make me fall. Nothing you say can tear me down. I know what I believe, Rune, and I will exact upon them their own punishment. This is my mission. You know as well as I do that I'm the one who will go down in history as a hero, no matter the means I use. You will go down as a man who was too afraid to fight." Cipher paused. "My suffering has become so great that it justifies any and every way of making my enemies spiral and crash to the ground," he spat.

"I'm not afraid," Rune said softly and firmly as he stared his brother down, "but I do value life. I value the fact that people can change. I understand that it's not my place to make the decision to end a life or cast it into the depths of oppression."

"Look around you, Rune! These people haven't changed for hundreds of years." He yanked the sleeve up his right arm, revealing his red-and-black mark. "They define me by this one simple mark, that should have no inherent negative meaning. If they don't see it, they don't know the difference. Their minds are so closed, they won't even face the fact that the "logic" supporting this system doesn't make sense at all."

"I know that just as well as you, if not better! I lived in the open in Akayta for two more years than you," Rune replied.

"I have experiences I never even told you about, Rune. There are too many of them to count. I'm not willing to go through anything like that again. Remember when I was away from home for four days?"

"Of course. I was going out of my mind with worry. I searched the city for you five times, not stopping, even when night fell," Rune said with the pain of remembrance of a time when the threads of trust were yet unbroken.

In that moment, Astrid caught a flash of change in Cipher's eyes. They softened for a split second and revealed a deeply rooted love for his brother. And a piercing heartache.

But he hid it behind a frightening storm of anger that rolled over his eyes once again. It broke Astrid's heart to realize that if he just let himself see clearly, he would break through that wall and choose the right path. She hoped with every inch of her being that he would open his eyes, let the anger go, and choose to be free.

Cipher continued, "That day a group of eight firstborns beat me until I was unconscious. They ridiculed me, then left me for dead. When I woke up outside the city three hours later, I couldn't remember a thing. Not a single detail of who I was or where I had come from. It was the most terrifying experience of my life. I sat there those four days trying to remember something. I was too disoriented and terrified to get up and return to the city. Do you know what it's like to forget your entire life? It was frightening beyond words. Finally, my identity came back to me and I made it home. That's just one example of the pain the Akaytans caused me."

"We've all felt that pain. But Astrid and I approach it differently. We forgive."

"You seem to think you understand her. You think that she loves you. The truth is that I understand her deepest desires more than you ever will. I am carrying out the secret desires that she's afraid you will reject. You were the friend that talked to her, but I've watched her for just as long as you have and I know her better."

"You know nothing of what she thinks. I found her crying in Velee because of your stilted views and an assassination *you* planned."

As his words rang through the water and Astrid watched their intensity, her mind wasn't processing the fact that they were talking about her. It was like she was watching from the outside, and didn't know the person of whom they spoke. Glancing down at her timepiece she was shocked back into reality.

"You know that…" Cipher began.

"Stop fighting! We only have two hours before the core explodes, I believe a truce was mentioned?"

Cipher took a deep breath, trying to calm down. "My truce is simple. I stop firing and you don't warn the Veleens about the core. I know you've already warned the Akaytans and they will warn the Veleens, but don't do it yourselves. It's all I ask." His voice was carefully controlled.

Stillness pervaded the space for several moments. Rune's and Astrid's minds raced as they exchanged looks. *We have to warn the Veleens.* She glanced at Cipher, who was studying their faces intensely. Then it dawned on her. She closed her eyes. *He wants revenge. He doesn't care about changing the oppressive rules in Akayta and Velee, he's interested in payback for all the times he suffered. For all the times* he *was abused in the name of false superiority.*

Her heart went out to him as every time she'd been mocked and hated flooded into her memory. *I understand, but there's a point where you have to forget and move on. That doesn't mean it's easy to forgive, but it's imperative.*

I have the feeling he's not going to just let the Akaytans escape either — he has something else planned. These people will die if we don't tell them. And it is much easier for him to forgive me than give back the lives of the thousands he'll kill.

She'd made her decision. In his anger, in his storm of hate and hurt, Cipher forgot one thing. She pointed her stun gun at him and fired.

CHAPTER TWENTY-EIGHT

The laser shot through the water. Cipher's face lit with surprise, but he realized what she had done too late. His eyes locked onto hers for a split second, then it hit him. His eyes closed and he floated to the floor. Rune glanced back toward the waiting contingents of fighters, who were hidden from view.

He looked at Astrid with raised eyebrows. "You're certainly decisive, there's no doubt about that."

She pocketed her stun gun and sighed. "We need to get into the ships quickly, then send the message to the Veleens so they have time to evacuate."

Rune looked back at Cipher's people. "The real question is what we're going to tell the Star."

"Why don't we just tell them the truth," she said quietly, looking into his eyes.

"They could start shooting at us when they realize that we've knocked their leader out."

Astrid shook her head. "They won't. They're a group of people who've been trained to follow since birth. They still don't fully understand that there's a place for making their own decisions.

"One of Cipher's shortcomings is that he trusts absolutely no one. He didn't have a second in command. His people still need to be saved. It's insidious. Persecution destroyed his ability to trust. He thinks any kindness you show someone will be mocked and disregarded. And now he thinks only of himself, only of revenge. That's what oppression does. That's how the victim becomes the inflictor." She closed her eyes. "And those of us who break out of the mold and have to be leaders, must fight our battles while trying to erase those residual effects. The battle goes on to make sure that we aren't acting the same way as the people we've seen all of our lives who've treated us badly."

"That's true." He took her hand. "Well, I can tell you for a fact that you've successfully evaded that trap," Rune replied gently and quietly.

The feeling of his hand, which was becoming familiar, made her smile. "So have you. We just have to keep moving forward."

He moved forward and bent his head closer to hers. She didn't have to wait, she didn't hesitate, she met his kiss. With all the buried hopes, dreams, and strength in her. With all of the expectations she had for herself. The sweetness, security, and love that they shared burned through her. She knew that they were in this together, until the very end. *I'm not alone anymore.*

CHAPTER TWENTY-NINE

They pulled away and after a silent moment Rune looked back at the waiting people.

"Anyway, I agree. We have to take the chance and hope they listen."

She sighed, "It's always about hoping they'll listen, isn't it?"

They swam back. Both groups were glancing at their timepieces then up at the couple. Frantic whispers started running through the Star.

When they got close enough, Astrid shouted to the frightened, dirty faces. She was reminded again how none of these people were meant to be soldiers.

"Rune lied to you all. His intent was not to help you form a peaceful society, his purpose was to exact revenge. Rune was sending out assassins to Velee. That is certainly not the start of a peaceful world. He even lied about his name." She motioned to Rune. "This is Rune. The person you were following is his twin brother, named Cipher. You may all believe me or you may not, but whatever the case, the core is going to explode in less than two hours. We have to evacuate. We stunned Cipher, but we'll get him off too. Work together and just get yourselves and the wounded onto the ships."

Most of the Star looked dumbfounded, but they started following her instructions. *There's so little time.*

As she directed the speedy search for the wounded and guided people into the ships, Astrid felt strangely calm. She realized that she was more sure of herself. She knew her role in that moment and felt a newfound confidence. A peace with herself that had been missing ever since she could remember.

Many were on board already and the last comb-through for survivors was underway. She looked down at her timepiece. *Ninety minutes.* She hastened her way to the white, round cabin of the smallest ship, which held the Star and Cover. Rune was there along with Dev.

He looked at her. "Are we ready?"

She gave a nod.

"Let's go," he told the pilot.

Dev nodded sharply, then pushed a button. Astrid was impressed by his calm focus and steady hand. The huge dome parted in the center, the sides descending to let the ship ascend. A thrill ran through Astrid as they started to rise. Her heart jumped as they paused just above the dome. Velee was spread out before them, and they were completely revealed. It was time to send the message.

Dev tapped on several buttons and waited for something. A look of confusion came over his face.

After a few seconds he quickly turned to them, his face pale as ice. "There's a malfunction with the system, Rune. The message is not being transmitted."

A sense of severe vulnerability crept over Astrid. Here they were above all of Velee, and the message wasn't being sent. If they stayed there too much longer the Veleens might stop them from leaving. *But we can't leave without sending the message. Can we?*

"Try again." Rune's voice was firm and his eyes alert. He too realized the danger they were in.

Dev pushed the buttons again and read several other instruments besides. As she watched his face, it suddenly hit her how young everyone was. They were carrying such responsibility, but Astrid had only just turned seventeen and Rune was only nineteen. People could change so much in so little time. Astrid would never have imagined that she would be sitting in a spaceship above Velee with Rune and her redeemed persecutor.

Dev turned back to them. "It's no use. I can't get it through." He paused and silence reigned for a moment. "What are we going to do now?" he asked with sudden anger and a hint of despair.

It had already been five minutes since they ascended out of the shiphouse. It wouldn't be long before the Veleen soldiers reached them. From her view she could see a large mass of merpeople entering the city. She assumed they were the Akaytans.

The responsibility weighed heavily on her, filling every bone in her body. Astrid decided on her course of action in that second. She bolted up, exiting the cabin.

"Where are you going?" Rune shouted after her.

Astrid darted through the ship, opened a small hatch, and exited. She swam down onto the stage in the town center where she had been poisoned. The cacophony of colored buildings and people met her eyes and ears. The ground was already trembling. Most people were scowling and arguing. Tremors were coursing through the water, gently shaking everyone. Vibrations hit her from all directions.

Astrid stood there quietly, no one taking notice of her at first. Time flowed in slow motion as the memory flashed back into her mind. These same people tried to murder her when she warned them about the core the first time. They might not listen this time either. Why should she risk her life for these people who had treated her so horribly?

Then she saw a pair of eyes that she remembered.

Delta.

The kindly mermaid who'd helped her the first time she came to Velee. As their eyes met and they stared at each other she thought, *I can't become like Cipher.*

As hard as it is, I must overcome and forgive. There is always room for a second chance.

She snatched a mic patch from the case on stage and faced the crowd. "Listen! Do you feel those tremors? The core is going to explode in only seventy minutes. You didn't believe me last time, but I'm telling you again. You have to evacuate." Eyes turned to her blankly, then small gasps of panic arose as they looked down at the ground and gradually realized she was telling the truth.

With every word, Astrid was overcoming the unforgiveness she hadn't realized existed inside her. Her voice faltered at first, but then it grew louder and stronger. She knew what she had to do and she was doing it. A sense of the power in this purpose rippled over her.

She shouted as loudly as she could manage, "You have to hurry. Don't push, there is room in the ships for everyone. You must go now. Don't go back for any of your possessions. Just get onto the ships. Figure the rest out later."

Astrid watched as understanding dawned in the surrounding eyes. They followed her directions without delay and started rushing to the shiphouse. A gigantic commotion arose as the merpeople swam far and fast and zipped by on transports.

She swam down through the streets and continued shouting her message, guiding people to the shiphouse. Time spun by like it had never been constant. She pointed both Akaytans and Veleens the right way. They pushed past her in waves heading toward their escape. It felt almost like a dream. Water and bodies crushing together, rushing past in panic.

Finally she looked around and realized that no one remained in the streets. It was so quiet and still, every open door seemed eerie. She looked up toward the ships, many of which were rising through the atmosphere into space.

One remained. The small ship that held the Cover and the Star. She'd accidentally moved farther away from it than she realized. The waves from the shaking core coursed through the water. She hovered there, the only moving thing outside of the ships. Even the pest fish had taken cover.

It only took her a second to realize that she had to get back to the ship. A figure leaned out of the hatch. Rune. His eyes were panicked as his arm waved for her to hurry. Her head whipped to her timepiece. Three minutes. Shock ran through her. She hadn't been watching the time. Her mind only took a millisecond to calculate that if they waited for her, they would still be in the atmosphere when the planet exploded. *They will all die if they wait for me.*

She was calm. In that moment Astrid made a decision. *For Rune, for Honor, for Ris, even for Cipher.* She straightened her back and clenched her fist. Then she held it straight up in the air. She could barely see Rune's face, but she still did.

As he realized what she was doing, he shouted. "Astrid! No!"

The sound carried to her ears, but she kept her fist in the air. They were watching for the signal, and in the stillness of everything else, they saw it. Hands pulled him inside and closed the hatch while the ship rose through the water towards space. The tremors were rumbling through the water with a new intensity. As the ship shimmered and disappeared from her view, Astrid was left alone on the dying planet. One individual in a vast space. Her fist still outstretched as she stared into space.

An impression placed itself into her head. *You are not alone.* All of a sudden, understanding and the joy of something she didn't know before enveloped her.

"God, you're here," she whispered.

Then the planet exploded. The cadence of the melions had finally become so unrestrained that they destroyed themselves.

CHAPTER THIRTY

Rune rushed to the window as the ships pulled out of the atmosphere and into space. They weren't that far from the planet when it exploded. The silent sound shook everything with a blinding fury. In a brilliant burst of light, blue masses of water shot through space in all directions creating a sparkling mosaic of destruction. The ships were just barely out of it reach.

With every second he stared out the window, Rune's heart broke a little more. "Astrid," he whispered. *No. I need her. She can't be gone.*

Rune could barely form a thought, he was too overwhelmed with emotions. Tears poured from his eyes uncontrollably as sobs wracked his body. The image of her floating there with her fist in the air and that tranquil look on her face blanketed his mind's eye. He understood why she did it. But it hurt too badly. She died to save the rest of them. The Veleens and Akaytans, the Star and the Cover. She gave her life to save those who'd mistreated her.

He clenched his teeth and closed his eyes as he sat right up against the window. There were others around, but they didn't register in his mind. All he felt was the pain rising in his heart. He hadn't realized how deeply she was implanted in his thoughts. Whenever he tried to think of something else, everything led back to her.

Suddenly the voices about him started mounting in excitement. He was forced to glance up. However much he wanted to be left alone, he was still their leader. He was still responsible.

Whispers ran through the water as people crowded around the windows. He looked out his own.

A spinning blue oval of light had appeared in a patch of water floating away from the planet. Then it disappeared and in its place was a flash of gold and red...His mouth opened in disbelief.

Astrid?

At first his brain didn't register what he was seeing. There she was, floating in space. He could tell by her face that she was struggling. She was floating in a drifting patch of water—the only thing keeping her alive—and it was rapidly dispersing. *She won't be able to breathe,* he realized. Rune bolted up and raced through the ship. He strapped a small silver rectangle to his back that attached to a mask, which went over his mouth.

His heart raced. Every second could be the difference between life and death for her. Once he activated the waterlock and pulled on a spacesuit, he exited the ship into space.

There she was. *Astrid. Oh, Astrid.* He had never known what it was like to hear his heartbeat in his own ears. It was strange because the sound came from so deep inside. His eyes didn't move from Astrid as he made his way toward her form as quickly as he could. She was outlined by the blackest black, and the sparkle of the stars. Her eyes moved to him as he took her in his arms and they were both pulled back toward the ship by those inside. Her face was deep shade of purple, but she gave a little smile, even as she tried to draw breath when there was nothing to draw in.

Everything in him belonged to her. She was his only focus. He didn't glance as the enormous space filled with twinkles of light. He didn't glance at the dead planet which had once been his. He didn't glance at the ethereal and biting white sun. He only watched her face. He felt like he was choking with her.

Within a moment they were back in the ship and the hatch was closed.

Water rushed into her lungs so quickly that Astrid almost choked as she gasped it in and out. Spots filled her vision and her mind was foggy, but it soon started to clear. Her breathing slowed to normal and her face returned to its natural color.

"Are you alright, Astrid?" Rune's soft voice entered her mind and she realized that he was still holding her. His words were simple, but his voice was filled with such incredible relief. She clasped him in her arms in response. They stayed that way for who knows how long. Tears of joy cascaded through the water as she tightened her arms around his neck. *Everyone is safe.*

Safe. At that moment it was the best word in the world to her. She turned her face to Rune and their smiles and eyes communicated without speaking. There are some emotions that would take hundreds of words to explain, but can be understood in one glance. The joy and relief she felt was overwhelming in such a glorious way.

She slowly stood up. Mermaids and mermen rushed around her with excitement, asking all kinds of questions and congratulating her.

Among the faces she spotted Honor, who gave her a small smile. It would take her time to heal, but she would.

She also spotted Ris, whose joyful eyes had been sobered by the experience, but who she hoped would also recover eventually.

Tears of absolute amazement and relief continued to pour forth. She glanced at the massive expanse of gorgeous space and stars that she'd never seen from this angle before.

Astrid parted from Rune and swam up a little bit so she could see everyone sitting in the compartment.

Then she grinned and shouted, "We have the chance to form a new way of living. No one will suffer under the government of our new people. It's time for a fresh start. We will be called the Dellinians, the Dalandian word for unity. We have to move forward and celebrate our new start."

A cheer rose and, in that moment, everything was brimming with light and discovery.

CHAPTER THIRTY-ONE

Astrid swam back down into the crowd, then floated there quietly as she watched the flurry of hugging and talking. It made her excited. *This is a chance we never would've had if Dalanda hadn't been destroyed.* Rune floated beside her.

He turned to her, "How did you get away?"

She gave him a quick glance, unsure of what to say. "Here. Let's go somewhere more private."

He nodded, guiding her down an empty, white hall. Both sides were lined with doors which Astrid assumed were apartments. She turned to face him and tried to figure out how to begin.

"It's hard to explain. You'll just have to follow me the best you can and then I'll clarify." She took a deep breath. "Several months ago, Effie made a discovery. While studying an ancient Atoan book, she realized there was a code hidden within the text. When she deciphered it, she found something unbelievable.

"It turns out that inside the DNA of every Dalandian is a fixed gene that gives us the ability to time-travel. But we can only travel through holes in the timestream. Effie did research and observed the phenomenon. When I left, she gave the notes to me for safekeeping.

"Well...just a moment before Dalanda exploded, I saw a spinning, blue light—a timestream hole. It opened right on top of me, and then I was floating through a place filled with so many colors and forms. It was strange. It didn't feel like any time was passing, but I knew I was moving. I could've been there for millions of years or one second.

"Anyways, then I fell out of another hole that formed in a mass of water which was drifting away from the planet.

"I found out about time-travel several weeks ago, but I didn't tell you before because it would've put you in danger. Effie was threatened and I was attacked because we possessed the knowledge of time-travel. I'm telling you now though since I think we're safe."

Rune was quiet and thoughtful as he nodded.

"Something happened, Rune. Right at that moment, I thought I was going to die. Then, it was revealed to me. There is someone who is always with us; there to help us. Someone who created everything. The one who gives us the hope that life doesn't end at death. I felt such a sense of peace. It was God, Rune.

"The odds of a continuance hole appearing right in front of me on Dalanda and then near the ship, right when I needed them to, are statistically impossible. Continuance holes can only appear in water. The one I came out of was in drifting water from the planet. I was rescued," Astrid said with conviction.

Rune looked at her with confusion. "Don't tell me you started believing in the Sirof. Astrid…"

Astrid laughed. What she'd experienced was the opposite of everything the Sirof stood for. It wasn't some religion dreamed up to keep a caste system in place. It was tactile and real, something she could feel and touch. Something that interacted with her. Something that saved her— in more than one way, perhaps.

"No, no, no. This is *real* Rune. Not the Sirof. There *is* something more than we can see, it just wasn't what the Akaytans thought it was. I'll talk with you about it more later."

He gave her an uncertain glance.

She pulled him into a hug. "Trust me, Rune. We both know there's more to life and death than we could possibly imagine, and I think we're about to discover it. There's a greater plan to the rhythm of the universe. A design. Who gave you your sense of right and wrong? Who created all of this? God is the opposite of the Sirof. He's the way to freedom, not chains. Don't be afraid," she whispered.

He hugged her tighter and nodded into her shoulder.

It would take Rune time to get over his fear of the chains he associated with religion, but Astrid knew that eventually he would understand. She was a student as well, so they could learn together.

At that moment a man swam up and asked Rune to come review their supplies with him.

He glanced back at Astrid, "Are you feeling alright?"

She smiled, "Yeah, go ahead."

Astrid watched until she was left alone in the white, curving hall. The red pouch around her waist that held her possessions was too tight. She unbuckled, then opened it.

The first thing she saw was Honor's small copy of *Time's Grudge*. She took it in her hand and brushed her fingers over its beautiful cover. *I'll go return it. I want an excuse to talk to her anyways.*

The warning that Honor gave right before she left the Star resounded in her head. Astrid also wanted to check to see how her friend was doing.

As soon as she reached the common area, she scouted Honor out. Amid the bubbling excitement and flurry of talking, Honor sat alone in a far corner, staring out the window. It struck Astrid's heart. She swam over and sat down by her friend.

"Hi."

Honor looked up in surprise. Her tired eyes brightened a bit as she said, "Hi."

Astrid looked down at the book in her hands, then handed it to Honor. "I haven't had a chance to read it, but I thought I'd better return it to you before I lose it for good."

Honor smiled as she took the book. Then her smile fell as she gazed up at Astrid. "Almost all of our books, all of our art has been destroyed. All of our history is gone. No one had time to save much of it. I'm not sure about Akayta and Velee, but all of the digital books in Fillerra were on a server that was destroyed." She looked down at the book in her hands. "This may be the last shred of Dalanda."

"Our history isn't gone. We're the product of it and it lives in our memories. We can write down the stories we've read for future generations. As for the art and fiction, it is lost. But we get to start over and create a new culture, with our own art. It hurts, but sometimes it's necessary to start over."

A tear escaped from Honor's eye. "I know. But it's so hard. I already lost Fillerra, now I have lost all of Dalanda."

Astrid gave her a side hug and sighed. The waves of loss were crashing down on her head as well. "We just need to try to think of the future. Maybe one day someone will look back on us and be inspired, just as you are inspired by the characters in history. Dark times like these are when we have to believe in the future, believe that the door to light is only a few feet away."

Honor bit her lip as she pulled a parcel of palare out from her messenger bag. "I took your suggestion and am writing my story down."

"Is it helping?"

"Yes. I feel better with every word I write. I know that my mind won't be Fillera's last foothold of memory."

"The memories of Dalanda are in all of our minds, and we will no doubt write our history down for the future." She paused. "There's something I'm curious about. You were warning me the day I left. I didn't miss it. How did you know?"

Her eyes saddened. "As you know, I was the records keeper, therefore I learned about all of the various types of missions and assignments Cipher had been giving out. He needed help with administration and he didn't want me to leak the information outside of the complex. That's why I didn't receive an assignment. He knew I was against him from the moment I saw those assassination orders. I couldn't get out, Astrid. I was trapped in the complex and I couldn't tell anyone else there, because I, conveniently, also happened to know that he had cameras everywhere. He didn't mind having one person who knew everything, as long as I was controlled by fear. He just wanted...no needed, a group of people who actually trusted and wanted to obey him."

"That really shouldn't shock me, but it does."

"There's more. A lot more. It's so hard to even know where to start." She paused for a moment then continued, putting emphasis on her next words, "He controlled all of the tribes, Astrid. Both of them. Akayta and Velee."

"What?" she asked, blinking with disbelief.

Grief and tiredness showed in the lines around Honor's eyes. "He was controlling their leaders through fear, and they were doing whatever he demanded. He used the assassinations and the threat that he possessed a super weapon to gain a hold and keep it.

"He was torturing them through terror, then his plan was to take over completely and make them slaves. The reason he gathered the Star was so that he could have a small army of people who would take orders directly from him, not the leaders. He guessed that outcasts would be somewhat easier to control, because of the submissive mentality pounded into them from the time they were children. Cipher worked to attract the vulnerable. Those desperately searching for love and acceptance. He took advantage of them, Astrid.

"He was worried that the Akaytans or Veleens would try to fight back. And that's exactly what the Veleens did when they attacked the complex. Cipher told the Veleen high commander that he would pay if anything like that happened. He made good on his word. The Veleens attacked the complex, and so Cipher had him assassinated.

"Astrid. That's not all. He was planning on dropping a bomb on the Akaytans and Veleens once his ship took off safely. They are all safe right now because you took control. He would have gone through with it. I know he would." She looked down at her hands.

Astrid closed her eyes in horror. She worked to keep her breathing steady as bile rose in her throat. He was going to *kill* all those people. He was going to murder them simply because he felt like it.

In addition to that, Cipher had used the Star as nothing more than soldiers. People to die for his personal whims. People who didn't know how to stand up for themselves. He took advantage of their oppression to satisfy his desire for revenge and power. Her horror bled into anger.

"He didn't."

"Oh, he did. It was torture, I couldn't help. I couldn't tell anyone without him killing me. I couldn't get out. And there was no way to contact anyone else."

Astrid shook her head in amazement. *Cipher's had been in control of Akayta and Velee for the past year. That also explains why he was waiting for us at the shiphouse. The Akaytans sent the message. They would've had a transmitter strong enough to send it that far.*

She paused awkwardly for a moment, wondering if she should ask a question that had been nagging at her. "Was there any rational reason to be wary of the machine in the Avocation Hall? Or was that just...I don't know."

Honor started nodding before she even finished her sentence. "It was a mind control machine. Once someone spent three hundred hours in it, they would be programmed to obey only one person. That person was Ciphcr. It uses addictive agents to keep you coming back. Cipher was frustrated that it would take so long to brainwash someone, but it was the best model he could find on the Veleen Black Market. I know because I saw the transaction records.

His plan had three phases. One: get control of the Akaytan and Veleen leaders through threats and violence. He wanted to torment them with fear of a weapon from Cog, while waiting for the Star to come completely under his control. Two: he would stage a military takeover in the open and create radical changes. He was going to make the Akaytans and Veleens suffer in all the ways he suffered. Three: eventually he *was* going to leave with the Star for the "paradisal planet." It isn't necessarily the same as the planet in the Avocation Hall machine, but it does exist. As he left Dalanda, he planned to drop the bombs that would destroy the Akaytans and Veleens.

"I'm speechless."

Honor just shook her head slightly, her desolate eyes telling of her experiences with the Star.

Then she brightened a little and looked back at Astrid. "But that is over. We don't have to worry anymore."

The magnificent burden Honor had been carrying lifted as the realization dawned on her. She laughed lightly as tears came to her eyes and she quickly swiped them away.

The corners of Astrid's mouth lifted. "That's what I've been trying to tell you."

Honor smiled, truly smiled, for the first time in a long while.

CHAPTER THIRTY-TWO

Cipher sat in the cafeteria on the ship.

He'd woken up in a room guarded by a member of the Cover. The last thing he remembered was Astrid shooting him. When he asked the guard, he learned that the core had indeed exploded, and he now resided on a ship with the Star and the Cover. He also learned that Astrid died, which had shocked him into silence. He could barely begin to reconcile his present situation, but with that added information, he couldn't think straight.

Later he learned that she survived, but he still didn't know what to do with himself. He pushed down any remorse he felt, instead focusing on the anger about being held captive by his brother and the disappointment and frustration of his failure.

Now, he was sitting in the cafeteria, just like everyone else. Except for the fact that his guard ate with him, staring at him wide-eyed. Cipher examined the faces around him, trying to take in the sudden change in his position and the new surroundings. He saw many familiar faces of the Star, who all turned their gazes elsewhere when he looked their way. Faces he had never truly bothered to see, because he didn't want to.

There were also the many new faces—those from Rune's rebellion. Astrid and Rune sat on the other side of the room, laughing with their friends. His gaze drew Astrid's eyes for a brief moment. She gave him a sympathetic, pleading look.

He could read her expression as clearly as if she was talking to him. She was asking him to apologize, to reform himself. To stop hating. It was her nature, but it wasn't nearly as easy for him. He couldn't just forgive everyone who'd ever hurt him. The wounds went too deep for that. He fought to remember all the reasons he'd carried out such violent actions as his sense grand purpose ebbed away. Rune either couldn't see him, or was ignoring him. Neither of them had come to sentence him or talk to him...Cipher turned his head in anger and continued scanning the sea of faces.

He did a double take. A face he recognized all too well.

Dev.

Rage burned through him. He stood up abruptly, but sat down again when his warden gave him a challenging look.

How could Rune associate with such a...violent, evil person? Rune, who championed the cause of the oppressed. Yes, he'd always been opposed to violence, even against the golds. But...he couldn't have allowed Dev to become part of his tribe, could he? Yet Dev wore the Cover colors. How could Rune betray him in such a deep way?

He pressed his hands into the table and glared at Dev in disbelief. The wretched, horrible irony. Here he was, a prisoner of his brother, while one of the very golds who'd mistreated and humiliated him was free. Was respected, while he was ignored.

Dev saw him staring. He looked back down at his food in shame. Confusion settled over Cipher for a moment. That shame on Dev's face would never have even considered alighting there when Cipher knew him.

Cipher narrowed his eyes. What had caused this apologetic attitude? Dev glanced up at him again. He pushed aside his food, then made his way to Cipher's table and sat down.

"Can you watch him for a few minutes while I go get some food?" the guard asked. Dev nodded.

The guard left and Cipher laughed sarcastically, crossing his arms as he leaned back in his seat.

"Cipher. I'm sorry," said Dev.

"You had to come over here and gloat of course," he replied, putting on the cool, intimidating demeanor that he'd perfected.

"No," Dev shook his head. "I just came to say I'm sorry for how I treated you all those years ago. It was wrong. It was so wrong."

Cipher laughed bitterly. "Of course it was."

"Are you sure you know that?" he asked hesitantly.

"What?"

"Are you sure you understand that it was wrong? I heard about your plan. Everyone knows now. *That's* wrong... and yet you were about to do it."

"That wouldn't have been wrong, it was…" Cipher fought himself, trying not to give in to the remorse, trying to remember all the reasons he hated the ones. All the reasons he hated Dev.

He looked into his reformed oppressor's eyes, and it made him want to scream. There was no more malice towards him there. Nothing to fight against. Only repentance.

Suddenly his thirst for revenge against Dev, against the ones seemed...empty. In panic, he let rage fill his mind with its corrupting current, overpowering those emotions which threatened to break down his resolve. He didn't *want* to feel again.

"Something happened to me, Cipher. I realized how terrible my actions were." Dev's voice broke, "I changed. That part of me was ripped away and remade into something else...when I let it happen. What I'm saying is that you don't have to let your past actions determine who you will be for the rest of your life. Or my past actions..." he said. "I'm sorry. That's what I'm telling you. Please don't let my old hatred define you. Please, Cipher. I've changed and you can too," he said solemnly.

"My sister was murdered by a one! Murdered by a man like you. I have plenty of reasons to be angry. I have plenty of reasons to seek vengeance," Cipher said, raising his voice.

Dev locked eyes with him. "My younger sister was murdered by a one as well. It caused me to see the error of my ways. And change. You have the choice." Dev got up, and moved back to his old spot as the guard returned.

Cipher was speechless. He allowed his anger to rule him. Cascading over him as an old friend.

But a steady tide of emotions, ushered in by Dev's words, were crashing against that wall of rage, breaking it down.

CHAPTER THIRTY-THREE

Cipher sat in his room, arms crossed, trying not to think. If he started thinking, then he would come to an emotional conclusion he didn't want to face: he was wrong. He'd been cruel and malicious, he'd disregarded life and everything important for money— for the want of power. Stupid, meaningless power. There was no triumph in that...none. He shook his head, forcing himself to stop thinking about it.

He was still clinging onto that last shred of hatred. If he didn't have that, who was he? A hero? That thought was laughable. Impossible. A coward? Most likely.

If he turned his back on his hatred Cipher would lose his pride because he would be forced to admit his brother was right. He would have no fin to stand on, no creed to identify himself with.

But his brother would hate him eternally either way. If the difference was only in his own mind and his own eyes, then what did he have to lose by destroying his enmity? More importantly, what could he gain?

At that moment Cipher realized that his sense of self had become enveloped in loathing and anger. They'd consumed him. He didn't want that. He wanted to be a person worthy of honor. Worthy of respect. But it was too late for that. Much too late.

Screams and clangs echoed down the hallway, startling him out of his thoughts. The door flew open and Dev, who'd been posted as a guard outside, hurled himself into the room, followed by laser fire. He banged the button that shut the door.

The hatch shook as if was being hit from the other side. Dev panted, staring at it in disbelief. His weapon hung loose in his hand.

"What's happening?" Cipher shouted over the din outside.

"The-the other Dalanadans are attacking us. They're boarding."

"They're boarding?" Cipher asked in shock.

Dev nodded grimly. He closed his eyes, took a deep breath, and then headed towards the door.

He paused, then turned back to Cipher and met his eyes.

"We need everyone on our side fighting. What do you choose?"

They stared at each other. Dev understood the war Cipher was fighting with himself. He was giving him a chance. And that was all Cipher needed to let that one last string of hatred and fear and anger go.

"I'm ready. I forgive you, Dev," he replied steadily.

Relief flooded him as well as remorse and sorrow. He understood what he'd done, he was looking at it honestly for the first time, and it tore his heart out. But now...there was the relief of no enmity. He hadn't realized how much it'd been weighing on him, eating away at his soul.

There was silence for a moment, then Dev smiled and handed him a gun. "Let's do this."

With that, he opened the door. Lasers zoomed everywhere, and swarms of angry people rushed about. It was a miracle that neither of them were shot. Cipher barely had a second to think before dodging another lethal laser. One after another, he stunned the attackers. They were disorganized. Cipher perceived this fact easily enough. It gave him a small bit of comfort. Many had a crazed look in their eyes. Their world had changed so quickly. They were desperate and confused and they didn't want it to change. This was no well-organized assault. Adrenaline pounded through his head. His eyes remained focused as he and Dev were able to hold their position in the hall, incapacitating a fair number of the attackers.

The hallway was finally clear. Without a word, they both hurried toward the bay. Surely enough, the other ship was connected to the mouth of the bay, creating a wide-open doorway between them.

Cipher's eyes rapidly swept the area, searching for the controls. Once he spotted them, he rushed over and closed the doors.

"I managed to undock the other ship," said Dev as he flipped a series of switches on the control panel.

"Good job. We need to find out what's happening in the rest of the ship," Cipher stated. Dev nodded and they made their way through the hallways, laser guns ready, eyes alert. They rushed towards the sound of fire in the large command room ahead.

A battle was raging, but Cipher could see that it was winding down, just like the battle in the hall. He spotted Astrid and Rune, panting, next to each other— as he'd noticed they always were. Only a few more. Rune's eyes briefly flashed with surprise when he caught sight of Cipher, but he turned away, focusing on another target.

Astrid's eyes, on the other hand, were trained on him. She froze and he cringed at the horror on her face. Cipher's eyes were drawn to an upper class Akaytan and where the end of his gun was pointed. It happened so quickly that Cipher had no time to think and Astrid certainly had none, as she saw it a moment after him. Cipher didn't hesitate for a split second.

He shouted, "No!" and fired at the man who was about to kill his brother.

Astrid gasped, Rune whipped around, his eyes alert, swiftly perceiving what had nearly happened as the man slipped to the floor. Only a few more, and finally the only conscious people in the room belonged to the Star or the Cover. Astrid and Rune stared at him amid the fray of people suddenly talking and urgently trying to help their injured friends.

Dev stood by him, but his expression held no shock. Discomfort filled Cipher's veins. They all knew what had just happened. The tension rose as Astrid and Rune glanced at each other in astonishment. Cipher had just saved Rune's life.

Cipher could see Dev smiling out of the corner of his eye. In that moment, he didn't want to look his brother in the face. Memories flooded back to him of joking and laughing with Rune.

What he'd done was unspeakable, and he hated the sadness, the shame that occupied Rune's eyes because of him. He didn't want to see it. Yes, Cipher had just saved him, but he knew they were now trying to assess whether he was a threat. Whether he'd only done it out of self-preservation. Finally, he braced himself and looked up.

Their eyes locked. Despite the buzz of chatter around him, Cipher's world was silent as he saw the sharpness, the confusion in Rune's gaze. He almost turned away, but then he saw those things give way to something else. Something he hadn't seen in a long time.

Love.

Rune's mouth turned up the slightest bit. Yes, there was pain, betrayal in those eyes, but there was also hope. Rune firmly placed his gun back in its holster.

Astrid was crying, but she was smiling too. Cipher sighed. *No, she will never be mine. But maybe that's alright*, he thought as they approached him.

As Astrid looked at him, he registered that this was the first time no fear or confusion were present in her countenance. Relief flooded through him at this realization.

"This isn't the end, Cipher. Not even close. This is the beginning," she said with a smile.

EPILOGUE

Some of the Akaytans and Veleens had considered their own ships too cramped, and therefore attacked. However, the attack was disorganized and an utter failure. Astrid and Rune still extended the invitation to join Dellinia, but they generally refused. Some decided to accept the offer, but most wanted to hold onto their practices of oppression, and couldn't even fathom a different world. So they parted ways.

It was a hard few weeks in those ships, with little food and water. By the time they got to Earth, Cipher's "paradisal planet," they were half-starved.

Astrid led the Dellinians along with Rune, and they eventually got married. They explored time-travel in greater depth and forged a shining new civilization, while observing and helping their human neighbors.

Cipher chose to continue with the Dellinians. He generally kept to himself when it came to strangers, but slowly pieced the relationship with his brother back together. It was a struggle for him, always fighting against his darker desires. Making a conscious effort every single day to be honest and kind. It was never easy and he made mistakes, but he'd made his choice. His history was rarely mentioned. The children of the Dellinians knew him as a quiet, responsible man. Most never guessed at his dark past. Anyone would tell you he was a hard worker who threw all his effort into any project he thought would contribute to the community. Forgiveness was given by many who lived through his crimes.

Ris recovered from her experience with Cipher and the war and continued to be a light with her positive outlook.

Honor became the official Dellinian historian. She would sit at her desk for hours writing down the history she remembered—and the new history that was being created day by day, project by project. Astrid was her closest friend. Someone she could truly trust. That meant the world to Honor. As she forged new friendships, she found she wasn't alone anymore.

Astrid persevered even when things seemed toughest. She never thought of herself as a hero, though many others did. Eventually, she became legend, though her story never lost its truth or became tarnished by exaggeration. Ultimately, it was lovingly painted onto the walls of the Dellinian cave where a girl named Gale saw it thousands of years later, and wondered if Astrid had gone through any of the same struggles.

In ways that she couldn't even begin to imagine, Astrid touched the lives of others and inspired them.

As she hovered over the stunning city of Dellinia, she marveled at the journey that had changed everything in a matter of years. *What a breathtaking thing born out of so much anguish. Silver is only one step from grey.*

VALIANT

Book Three of The Waterblaze Trilogy

Three time periods and legacies collide in the final installment of "The Waterblaze Trilogy." In the near future, Tivia, the leader of the Coalition, flees from a coup. Separated from her family with her young daughter by her side, she desperately searches for a way to keep the world from descending into chaos at the hands of Vire Quage. As a last resort, she pulls Gale and Force into her own time to help wage a war she can't fight alone.

When Astrid takes an experiment too far, she is flung into the future along with Cipher and Rune. There she meets Tivia and joins her cause.

Consequences for an experiment gone awry. A struggle to rise out of the wreckage. A family in danger. How much will Tivia sacrifice to save those she loves?

ACKNOWLEDGMENTS

To Mom and Dad: Thank you for always being there to listen. All those long hours spent discussing this process were worth it. I love you, Mom. You will always be my editor extraordinaire. Thank you Lisa for the incredible cover!

ABOUT THE AUTHOR

China Dennington is eighteen and loving it. She is a student at Emory University in Atlanta, Georgia who plans on studying the wonders of history. Her passions include God and upholding women's rights. To keep up with her newest releases follow her at www.ChinaDennington.com.